don't worry
life is easy

Also by Agnès Martin-Lugand:

Happy People Read and Drink Coffee
(Les gens heureux lisent et boivent du café)

don't worry
life is easy

*(La vie est facile,
ne t'inquiète pas)*

Agnès Martin-Lugand

Translated from the
French by Sandra Smith

WEINSTEIN
BOOKS

Printed in the United States of America.
Book design by Cynthia Young
Set in Adobe Caslon Pro

Library of Congress Cataloging-in-Publication Data
is available for this book.

ISBN: 978-1-60286-304-0
E-Book ISBN: 978-1-60286-305-7

Published by Weinstein Books,
an imprint of Perseus Books, LLC,
a subsidiary of Hachette Book Group, Inc.
www.weinsteinbooks.com

Weinstein Books are available at special discounts for bulk purchases in
the U.S. by corporations, institutions and other organizations. For more
information, please contact the Special Markets Department at Perseus
Books, 2300 Chestnut Street, Suite 200, Philadelphia, PA 19103, call (800)
810-4145, ext. 5000, or e-mail special.markets@perseusbooks.com.

First Edition

10 9 8 7 6 5 4 3 2 1

For my three men . . .

The success of a normal period of mourning is in no way forgetting the one who died, but the ability to allow him to take his correct place in a story that has ended, the ability to fully take part once more in the activities, plans and desires that give life its meaning.

—Monique Bydlowski, *Je rêve un enfant*

Don't worry. Life is easy.

—AaRON, "Little Love"

don't worry,
life is easy

1

How could I have given in to Felix yet again? I don't know how he miraculously always manages to win me over: he finds a logical argument or some other way to encourage me to go out. And I let myself be tricked into it every time, thinking that maybe something might happen to make me change my mind. But I know Felix as if he were my own flesh and blood, and our tastes are completely opposite. So whenever he thought or decided anything for me, he was completely and utterly wrong. I should have known that, we'd been friends for so long. But here I was, for the sixth Saturday night in a row, spending time in the company of a complete imbecile.

The week before, I'd been treated to someone who championed organic food and healthy living. You would have thought that Felix had totally forgotten the vices of his best friend. I'd spent the entire evening getting lectured about smoking, alcohol, and my terrible eating habits. That upper-class health freak in thongs had told me quite calmly that my lifestyle was disastrous, that I'd end up sterile, and that I was unconsciously causing my own demise. Felix must have forgotten to give him the technical specs of his potential girlfriend. Giving him my biggest smile, I told him that I actually knew a great deal about death and the temptation of suicide. Then I left.

The idiot of the day was a different type: rather good-looking, a respectable background, and not prone to lecturing. His flaw—a rather large one—was that he seemed convinced he could get me into bed by telling me tales of his conquests in the company of his mistress, otherwise known as his camera, the GoPro: "This summer, my GoPro and I slid down an icy mountain torrent . . . Last winter, my GoPro and I went skiing . . . You know, the other day, I tried the metro with my GoPro," etc. It lasted more than an hour; he was incapable of saying a single sentence with talking about it. I was at the point of wondering whether if he took it to the bathroom with him.

"Do I go where with my GoPro? I don't think I understand," he suddenly stopped and asked.

Oh, dear . . . I'd been thinking out loud. I was sick and tired of being seen as the evil woman who was incapable of showing any interest in what she was being told and wondering what she was doing there. Nevertheless, I decided to rip off the Band-Aid all at once.

"Listen, you're certainly a very nice guy but you're too much in love with your camera for me to come between you. I'll pass on dessert. And I'll have coffee at home."

"What's the problem?"

I stood up; so did he. I gave him a little goodbye wave and headed for the cash register; I hadn't become so unsociable that I would stick him with the bill for our fiasco. I glanced at him one last time and stifled the urge to burst out laughing. I was the one who should have had my GoPro to capture the look on his face. Poor guy . . .

The next day, my telephone woke me up. Who was daring to disturb my sacrosanct late sleep-in on Sunday morning? As if I needed to ask!

"Yes, Felix," I groaned into the phone.

"And the winner is?"

"Oh do shut up."

His chuckling got on my nerves.

"I'll expect you in an hour," he managed to say, "you know where." Then he hung up.

I stretched out in my bed like a cat before looking at my alarm clock: 12:45. It could have been worse. Though I had no difficulty getting up during the week to open my book café, Happy People Read and Drink Coffee, I did need to sleep very late on Sundays to recuperate, to clear my head. Sleeping remained my last indulgence; after being the refuge of my deepest sorrows, sleep now helped me through my little problems. Once I got up, I was happy to see that it was going to be a beautiful day: springtime in Paris had come to greet me.

When I was ready to leave, I stopped myself from picking up the keys to the bookstore; it was Sunday, and I had promised myself not to go there on the "Lord's Day of Rest." I took my time to get to the Rue des Archives. I strolled along, allowed myself to window shop a little while puffing on my first cigarette of the day, ran into some regular clients of the bookstore and gave them a little wave. This peaceful spell was broken by Felix when I arrived at our usual Sunday meeting place, a table outside a café.

"What the hell have you been doing? I nearly got kicked off our usual table!"

"Hello, my darling Felix," I replied, planting a sloppy kiss on his cheek.

His eyes narrowed. "You're up to something; you're being too nice."

"Not at all! Tell me about what you did last night. What time did you get home?"

"When I called you. I'm hungry; let's order."

I let him call the waiter to take our order for brunch. It was his new craze. To reassure himself, he'd declared that after his crazy Saturday nights, brunch would be better for him than some stale reheated pizza. Ever since then, he wanted me to be in attendance to admire him while he devoured his scrambled eggs, sausages, and bread along with a carton of orange juice that was supposed to quench his thirst the morning after.

As usual, I just picked at his leftovers; he made me lose my appetite. We leaned back comfortably in our chairs, smoking, our sunglasses perched on our noses.

"Are you going to see them tomorrow?"

"As usual," I replied, smiling.

"Give them a kiss for me."

"I will, promise. Don't you ever go anymore?"

"No, I don't feel the need to now."

"And to think I didn't want to set foot there before!"

It had become my Monday ritual. The bookstore was closed and I went to see Colin and Clara. If it was windy, if it rained, if it snowed, I went to them. I liked telling them about my week, all the little things that happened at the bookstore . . . Since I'd started dating again, I'd tell Colin all about my pointless fix-ups in great detail; I felt I could hear him laughing, and I laughed with him, as if we were co-conspirators. But it was much harder for me to talk to Clara about important things. My daughter . . . everything I remembered about her always made me sink into a pit of sadness. Without thinking, my hand rose to touch my neck: during one of my talks to Colin, I'd taken my wedding ring off the chain I wore. Took it off. Once and for all.

I'd worn nothing around my neck for months now. I'd explained to Colin that I'd thought about it and decided to accept Felix's suggestions about dating.

"You're with me, my love . . . and you'll always be with me . . . but you're gone . . . you're far away and will never come back. I've accepted that . . . but I want to try, you know . . . "

I'd sighed, tried to fight back the tears, and turned my wedding ring round and round in my hand.

"It's starting to weigh heavily . . . I know you won't hold it against me . . . I think I'm ready . . . I'm going to take it off . . . I feel that I've healed . . . I'll always love you, that won't change, but it's different now . . . I've learned how to live without you . . . "

I'd kissed the gravestone and taken off the necklace. My

eyes filled with tears and I let them flow. I'd squeezed my wedding ring with all my might. Then I'd stood up.

"See you next week, my loves. My Clara . . . Mama . . . Mama loves you."

Then I'd left and didn't look back.

Felix interrupted my thoughts by tapping my thigh.

"Let's go for a walk; it's nice out."

"Lead the way!"

We left to walk up and down the quayside. Like every Sunday, Felix insisted on crossing the Seine and making a detour to Notre Dame Cathedral to light a candle. "I have to repent for my sins," he'd say, but I was no fool: his offering was for Clara and Colin, his way of keeping a link to them.

While he paid his respects inside the church, I waited patiently outside, watching the tourists get attacked by the pigeons. I had just enough time to finish off a cigarette before seeing Felix act out his version of the death of the mother in the movie *Amélie*; it was worthy of an Oscar—especially the scream! Then the wonderful actor came and put his arm around me, waved to his imaginary cheering audience, and led me slowly towards our beloved Marais and the sushi bar we went to every Sunday night.

Felix was drinking sake. "You have to fight evil with evil," he said. As for me, I was happy with a Tsingtao. While eating some sushi, he began his attack and demanded a debriefing. It was going to be very brief!

"So, what's wrong with the one you went out with yesterday?"

"His camera's attached to his face!"

"Wow! That's really exciting."

I slapped the back of his head.

"When will you understand that we don't have the same ideas about sexuality?"

"You poor thing," he lamented.

"Should we go back? We'll be late for the movie on TV."

Felix walked me back to the door of the bookstore, as always. And gave me a big hug, as always.

"I have something to ask you," I said while still in his arms.

"What?"

"Please stop playing at Dating.com; I can't stand such awful evenings. It's so demoralizing!"

He pushed me away.

"No, I won't stop. I want you to meet someone nice and kind, someone you'll be happy with."

"You only introduce me to fools, Felix! I'll manage on my own."

He glared at me.

"Are you still thinking about your Irishman?"

"Stop talking nonsense! I've been back from Ireland for a year. Have I ever talked to you about Edward? No! He has nothing to do with this. It's ancient history. It's not my fault if you only introduce me to fools!"

"OK, OK! I'll leave you alone for a while, but you have to be open to meeting men. You know as well as I do that Colin would want you to have someone in your life."

"I know. And I intend to . . . Good night, Felix. See you tomorrow! It's the big day!"

"Yes!"

I gave him the same big kiss as a few hours before and went into my building. Despite Felix's objections, I didn't want to move. I liked living in my little apartment above the bookstore. I was at the heart of everything that was happening, and that suited me. But most importantly, it was here that I'd rebuilt my life all alone, with no one else's help. I took the stairs instead of the elevator and climbed up to the fifth floor. When I got inside, I leaned against the front door and sighed contentedly. In spite of our final conversation, I'd spent a wonderful day with Felix.

Contrary to what he believed, I never watched the movie on TV. I put music on—tonight it was Ásgeir, "King and Cross"—and began what I called my spa night. I'd decided to take care of myself, and when better than Sunday evening to make time to give myself a facial and all the other things we girls do?

An hour and a half later, I finally emerged from the bathroom, I smelled nice and my skin was soft. I washed down my last coffee of the day and curled up on the sofa. I lit a cigarette and let my thoughts wander. Felix never knew how much it had cost me to push Edward to the back of my mind so I wouldn't think about him anymore.

After I'd returned from Ireland, I hadn't kept in touch with anyone: not with Abby and Jack, not with Judith, and especially not with Edward. Obviously, he was the one I missed the most. The memory of him came back in waves, sometimes happy, sometimes painful. But the more time that passed, the more certain I was that I'd never hear from them again, and especially not from him. It would be pointless after so long; more than a year already . . . And yet . . .

About six months earlier, one Sunday in winter when it was pouring rain, I'd decided to clean out my closet. I came across the box where I'd put the photos he'd taken of the two of us on the Aran Islands. I'd opened it and melted when I saw his face. I rushed to the phone like a woman possessed, found his number in my contacts and dialed it. I wanted, no, I *needed* to know how he was. I was on the point of hanging up every time it rang, torn between the fear of hearing his voice and a deep desire to get back together with him. And he'd answered: just said his name, in his hoarse voice, then a beep. "Umm . . . Edward . . . It's me . . . ," I stammered, "It's Diane. I wanted . . . I wanted to know . . . umm . . . how you are . . . Call me back . . . please." After hanging up, I told myself I'd just done something really stupid. I'd walked all around the room, biting my nails. My obsession with knowing how he was, to find out whether he'd forgotten me or not, had kept me glued to telephone for the rest of the day. So much so that I tried again at ten o'clock. He hadn't picked up. When I woke up the next morning, I called myself all kinds of names when I realized how ridiculous I'd been. My moment of madness had made me understand that Edward no longer existed, he would remain just one episode in my life. He had started me on the path to free myself from my duty of loyalty to Colin. I felt free of him as well now. I was ready to open myself up to other people.

2

When I opened my eyes that Monday morning, I savored the importance of the day to come. That evening when I went to bed, I would be the sole proprietor of the book café, Happy People Read and Drink Coffee.

After my return from Ireland, it had taken me several weeks to decide to get in touch with my parents. I had no desire whatsoever to fight with them or to suffer their remarks about my lifestyle. When I'd finally called them, they invited me to come to dinner at the house, and I'd agreed. When I got to the family apartment, I felt ill at ease, the way I always did every time I went there. We didn't usually manage to communicate with each other. My father had remained silent and my mother and I beat around the bush without finding anything to talk about.

When we sat down to dinner, my father finally decided to speak to me.

"How's business?" he'd sneered.

His tone of voice and refusal to look at me put me on the defensive.

"I'm raising the bar, little by little. I'm hoping we'll be out of the red in about two months. I have ideas I want to put into place."

"Don't talk nonsense, you have no idea how to run the place. We've been telling you that since Colin died; he was the one who kept the bookshop going, as well as his regular job."

"I'm learning, Dad! I want to get there and I will!"

"You're not capable of it, which is why I intend to take things in hand."

"May I know how?"

"Since I doubt you'll find another man capable of doing everything for you, I'm going to hire a manager, someone strong and serious. If you want to go on playing at being the shopkeeper, I won't stop you. It will keep you busy."

"Dad, I'm not sure I understand . . . "

"I can see by the look on your face that you understand very well! Enough of this childishness!"

"You have no right!"

I stood up so quickly that my chair fell over.

"The bookstore is my home!"

"No, it's ours!"

I was fuming inside but deep down, I knew my father was right. They were the real owners of the bookstore: to give me something to do, they had taken out their checkbook, reassured and encouraged by Colin.

"Make a scene, if that amuses you," he'd continued. "I'm giving you three months."

I'd slammed the door and left. It was at that moment I understood that I'd changed, gotten stronger. Before, I would have been beaten down and gone through another depression. This time, I was determined, I had a plan. What they didn't know at the time was that I'd already started to put it into motion.

I'd gotten things back on an even keel, and I'd started by installing free Wi-Fi in the café. Thanks to that I'd attracted a student clientele—some of them spent the entire afternoon working in the room at the back. I'd also started given them a discount for coffee and beer to assure their loyalty. Most of them had gotten into the habit of buying their books from me, knowing that I was prepared to bend over backwards to find the biography they needed to salvage their term paper. And keeping regular opening hours had been successful: I always opened at the same time, unlike the days when Felix was the only one in charge. That had allowed me to create a reassuring atmosphere. No one ever found the door closed any more.

The three busiest times of the day were simple: in the morning when customers grabbed a quick coffee before going to work, at noon when the literary types had their lunch break—they were the ones who forgot to eat because they were looking for a new novel—and cocktail hour after work. That was when people came for a drink at the bar and every once in a while, they'd buy a book to keep busy on a night they'd be spending alone. Every now and then, I gave Felix free rein to organize a themed evening; there was no one better than him when it came to such events. He always found a speaker who was eccentric and unbelievably knowledgeable to discuss any theme arranged—and the debate was always controversial—which made the alcohol flow like water. So much so that the participants often left with several books under their arms, without really understanding what had been discussed. And Felix's tips were paid by promises of steamy nights. I never went to those evenings; they were his thing, the time when I let him have fun and closed my eyes to his avant-garde customers.

I had wanted the bookstore to become a warm, welcoming place, open to everyone, somewhere that all types of literature would find a home.

I wanted to advise readers while allowing them to enjoy themselves, to read the stories they wanted to, and without feeling ashamed. It didn't matter whether they wanted a literary prizewinner or a best-selling popular novel, only one thing counted: that our customers read, without feeling they were being judged because of their choices. Reading had always been a pleasure to me and I wanted the people who came to my book café to feel that, to explore, and, for those who were the most reluctant, to at least try it. All types of literature sat side by side on my shelves: detective novels, general literature, modern romances, poetry, books for young adults, biographies, bestsellers, and books for the most esoteric of readers. It was my own personal shambles, the place where Felix, my regular customers, and I came together. I loved the feeling it had of having to search through all the treasure to find *the* book. New clients were gradually initiated by each other.

Today, the bookstore was my equilibrium. It had allowed me to get my head above water, to resume my life in Paris, to realize the extent to which work was beneficial to me, to prove to myself—since I couldn't prove it to my parents—that I was capable of accomplishing something. Thanks to the bookstore, I had once again become someone blessed with relationships with other people; I was a woman who worked and took on responsibilities. I had to lose everything I loved the most to realize what tied me to this place, to these four walls. I hadn't taken a day off in a year; I was incapable of leaving and would never again let Felix run it alone.

The only failure in developing our business was not due to a lack of customers: it was my fault. I'd had the idea to start up reading workshops for children on Wednesday afternoons. Felix had encouraged me; he knew I loved children's literature. We'd done some publicity and distributed flyers in local schools, leisure centers, etc. I'd topped up my stock of fruit juices and especially my children's books. The big day had come. When I saw the first mothers coming in with their children, the little bell on the front door had made me jump for the first time in weeks; I'd hidden behind the bar. I just invited them to go to the little room in the back. I'd asked Felix to supervise getting them settled in while I went out for a cigarette. Since I was taking forever, he came out and told me they were waiting for me to start; I was the one leading the workshop. I staggered back inside to my little group. I'd started to read *The Blue Dog* and didn't recognize my own voice.

I realized I'd made a serious mistake when a little three-year-old boy came up to me. When I looked at him, I jumped back and started shaking all over. At that moment, it was Clara who I wanted to be coming over to me, to sit on my lap so she could see the book close up. Then I would have buried my nose in her hair. I dropped the book and called Felix to the rescue. It didn't take long for him to come over; he'd been standing there, watching me. He took over, playing the clown, and I went upstairs and locked myself in my apartment. I spent the rest of the day and all night rolled up in my quilt, screaming into my pillow, crying and calling out Clara's name.

The next day, the books were sent back to the publishers. That disaster made me realize something: I'd never get over losing my daughter. I could get over Colin, but not her. I'd realized that no child would ever come into my life again, or to the bookstore.

In spite of that incident, one decision had become essential. I'd made an appointment at the bank to review the situation on Colin's life insurance. He had taken every step to make sure I would want for nothing. I refused to squander any more of that money; it should be used for something important, something that would have made him happy. I had to find a project worthy of my husband. I'd already found it: I was going to buy the bookstore back from my parents.

We'd made it to the big day: ending these months of fighting with my parents. The importance of the day didn't stop me from visiting Colin and Clara. I walked down the paths of the cemetery smiling, with my head high. After putting down my armful of white roses, I twisted around so I could get down on my knees without looking ridiculous; I'd put on a black dress—it was a little tight—and high heels, which I hadn't done in ages. My parents had surely described me to the lawyer as irresponsible and depressed and I wanted to prove to them that I was totally the opposite.

"Today's the big day, my love! Tonight we'll be at our own place. I hope you're proud of me; I'm doing it for the two of you. And since I never do things by half, after we've signed the papers, I'll go out and celebrate with Felix! When I told him that, I thought he was going to cry tears of joy. Life is going on . . . it's strange . . . I can't be late; they need me to sign the papers! I love you both, my darlings. Clara . . . Mama . . . is with you . . .

I kissed their gravestone and left the cemetery.

The reading of the deed was carried out calmly and in silence. The big moment had come: the signing. I was shaking so much that I had to stop and start again. My emotions were surfacing: I'd succeeded, and all I could think about was Colin and the woman I'd become. When I sat down again, a few tears filled my eyes. I looked over at my mother: nothing. Then the lawyer handed me the document confirming that I now owned the property. The deed stated in black and white that I was a widow with no children. He politely told us we could go. Once we were out on the sidewalk, I turned towards my parents, looking for something without really knowing what.

"We didn't think you'd actually go through with it," said my father. "Try not to mess everything up, for once."

"I have no intention of doing that."

I looked at my mother. She came over to me and hugged me more warmly than usual.

"I never knew how to be the mother you needed," she whispered in my ear.

"That makes me sad," I replied.

"I'm so very, very sorry."

We looked into each other's eyes. I wanted to ask her "Why?" The look on her face told me she couldn't take my questions, my reproaches. My mother's armor cracked, as if she could finally deal with her remorse. But wasn't it too late? My father took her arm and said it was time to go. By way of encouragement, I was treated to "See you soon." They left on one side of the street and me on the other. I put on my sunglasses and headed for *my* bookstore. I walked down the Boulevard de Sébastopol to the Rue de Rivoli. I didn't take any shortcuts down the side streets: the wide avenues were calling out to me and I wanted to walk past the Hôtel de Ville and get jostled by the crowd by the BHV department store. When I finally took the Rue Vieille-du-Temple on my left, I was only about 100 meters from my bookstore. The moment the little bell rang, I told myself that Felix must have had informants on every street for he popped the cork on the champagne the minute I set foot inside. Champagne that sprayed all over the counter. Without bothering to pour me some in a flute, he handed me the bottle.

"You're amazing!"

I drank straight from the bottle. The bubbles tickled my taste buds.

"Shit! When I think that you're my boss now!"

"That's classy!"

"I prefer that to your father," he said, grabbing the bottle from me.

"Felix, you will always be a partner in my heart."

He crushed me to him and took a long drink.

"Shit, that stings!" he said, letting go of me, his eyes shining. "Teach me the joys of partying again!"

I didn't bother going upstairs to change. I wiped the champagne off the counter and closed up. Felix led me from one bar to another. Known as the white wolf, he went into each place as lord of the manor. The cocktails had been chosen in advance; my best friend had planned the evening in great detail. All his lovers and would-be lovers stood aside in a group to make room for me; if Felix loved me, they had to take care of me. Our journey was scattered with eccentric encounters, red carpets, sequins, flowers stuck into my hair, everything needed to make me a princess for a day. The mad atmosphere that Felix organized probably went to my head even more than all the alcohol I was served.

It was time to stop to eat. We went to a tapas bar for dinner, which certainly wasn't going to be enough to soak up everything we'd drunk. Our seats at the counter had been reserved. Felix knew very well that I loved sitting on high stools and seeing what was happening backstage. A bottle of red wine was opened for us. Felix raised his glass.

"To your parents, who won't be a pain in your ass anymore!"

I took my first drink without replying; the wine was strong, powerful, just like what I was feeling at the moment.

"I have no family left, Felix . . . "

He didn't know what to say.

"Do you see? Nothing is tying me to my parents anymore; I have no brothers or sisters. Colin and Clara are gone. You're all I have left. You're my family."

"Ever since we met at college, we were a couple, and that will never change."

"We've done everything together!"

"Except sleep together!"

A nightmarish vision for both of us! He put one finger in his mouth as if to throw up and I did the same. Like two teenagers!

"On the other hand, if you change your mind about having kids and don't find the right guy, I can make a donation at the sperm bank. I'll teach the kid about life."

I spit out my mouthful of wine and he burst out laughing.

"How could you suggest such a weird thing?"

"We were getting too sentimental and that bothered me."

"You're right! I want to dance, Felix."

"Your wish is my command."

We whizzed past the entire line of people waiting to get into the nightclub: Felix had his ins. He kissed the bouncer full on the lips right in front of my startled eyes. The last time I'd seen him such a state was at my hen party! A magnum of champagne was waiting for us in the VIP lounge. After knocking back two glasses, I was well on my way. I was swaying back and forth, eyes closed; I felt alive, ten years younger, free of my sorrows, and entitled to enjoy life.

"I made a request for you," Felix whispered in my ear. "Take advantage of it; they won't play it all night long."

Thanks to two pairs of arms, I was flown up onto the podium. The bass line and drums put me in a trance. Within minutes, I was the belle of the ball with "Panic Station" by Muse. For weeks now, I'd been listening to this piece of music nonstop, so much so that Felix couldn't take it anymore. He'd even caught me cleaning up the bookstore with this song playing in my headphones. I had an audience and I made everyone sing the chorus: *Ooo, 1, 2, 3, 4 fire's in your eyes. And this chaos, it defies imagination. Ooo, 5, 6, 7 minus 9 lives. You've arrived at panic station.*

Around four o'clock in the morning, by mutual agreement, we decided to head back home. The trip was a hard one, and annoying to anyone who was asleep. I kept howling out my song while Felix sang the chorus, a bottle of champagne stuffed into my jacket. He accompanied me to the door of the bookstore and glanced over at the shop window.

"Happy people control their own lives! This is your home now!"

"That's amazing!"

"Can you get upstairs by yourself?"

"Yes!"

We gave each other a big hug.

"Good night, my family," I said.

"Shall we keep going?"

"No way!"

I let go of him and opened the door.

"We're closed tomorrow morning, so go to sleep," I said.

"Thank you, boss lady!"

He left looking all perky, as if rejuvenated by the news he could sleep late. But what he didn't know was that I was planning on opening on time.

Getting up was horrible. Eyes half-closed, I looked around in my medicine cabinet and swallowed two Tylenols before having my first coffee of the morning. I took a cold shower so I could think clearly. As I was putting on my shoes, I realized the biggest mistake I'd made the night before wasn't having celebrated with Felix, but having kept my high heels on all night. I was going to have to work in thongs in April!

Like every morning, I took a shortcut to the bakery to buy the croissant and chocolate pastry I had every day. Then I opened the door to Happy People and left it open. The cool morning breeze would help me keep my eyes open—too bad about my frozen feet. I started the coffee machine and made myself a triple espresso. My early customers came in quietly and took their time to wake up with me by leafing through *Le Parisien* newspaper. Once the first wave of customers had gone, I tidied up whatever needed it, then looked over the stock, checked the accounts, and skimmed through the latest literary releases, as I'd done for almost a year. I knew I'd have a nice long quiet time because Felix's idea of sleeping late in the morning usually meant the afternoon. Let him enjoy it! Nothing had changed and yet everything was different. I had emerged as an adult, at peace with myself after the battle with my parents. I didn't owe them anything now. And life, my life, didn't depend on them, even if I did still feel a little bitterness.

3

At the end of this sunny day, I was leaning against the door-frame smoking a cigarette when a customer turned up. I glanced over at him—he didn't say anything to me; Felix could help him. When I got back inside, my partner was standing behind the counter, staring into space, and the customer seemed lost looking at the books and the way they were whimsically arranged. I walked over to him.

"Hello, can I help you?"

He turned toward me and paused for a moment. I gave him a little smile.

"Umm . . . hello . . . I think I've found what I needed," he said, grabbing a book at random. But . . . "

"Yes?"

"Are you still serving drinks?"

"Of course!"

"Then I'll have a beer."

He sat down at the counter, watched me fill his glass and gave me a little smile as a thank you. He started tapping on his phone. I discreetly watched him. This man gave off an air of assurance. He was attractive, but I couldn't decide if I would have turned around to look at him in the street. Felix cleared his throat, which brought me back to reality. The smile on his face annoyed me.

"What is it?"

"Can I leave you to close up by yourself? I'm expected somewhere . . . "

"No problem, but don't forget that tomorrow is delivery day, and I don't want to be left alone here, breaking my back again."

"What time?"

"Nine o'clock."

"You can count on me."

He grabbed his jacket, planted a kiss on my cheek and left. A few minutes later, my customer got a phone call that seemed to irritate him. While continuing his conversation, he finished his beer, stood up, and looked over at me to ask how much owed. He paid me, and asked his caller to hold on. He put his hand over the phone.

"Have a good evening," he said, "This is a nice place you've got here."

"Thanks."

He turned quickly around; the little bell on the door tinkled as he left. It made me smile. I shook my head and decided to close up a little early.

Of course, I was the only one there to accept the deliveries the next morning. To release my anger, I called Felix. It went straight to voice mail. "You're a pain in the ass, Felix! Once again I'm going to have to kill myself working alone!"

I begged the deliveryman to help me carry the boxes into the café, in vain. Shoulders drooping, I stared at the truck as it drove away down the street. I rolled up my sleeves and picked up the first box—the smallest one—when someone called out to me.

"Wait! I'll help you!"

The customer from the night before didn't give me time to react; he grabbed the box from me.

"What are you doing here?" I asked.

"I live in the neighborhood. Where should I put this?"

I led him into the storage room where I kept the surplus stock while continuing to question him.

"I've never seen you around before."

"That's because I just moved here three weeks ago. I noticed you . . . that first day, uh . . . I mean, your café . . . but I didn't have time to come in and have a good look around until yesterday. OK . . . should I bring the rest of the boxes in here, too?"

"No, that's OK, I can manage by myself. Don't make yourself late."

"Are you kidding?" he replied with a big smile before taking off his jacket and picking up the next package.

He was unbelievably efficient; everything was sorted out in ten minutes.

"All done! You see, it didn't take long."

"Thank you . . . Can you stay another few minutes?"

"Yes," he replied, without checking his watch.

"I'll leave you in charge for two minutes."

I rushed to the bakery and bought a bit more than my usual daily rations. My helpful customer hadn't moved when I got back to Happy People.

"Breakfast as compensation . . . how does that sound?"

"If you call me by my first name and treat me as a friend!"

I laughed and held out my hand.

"Diane."

"Olivier. Delighted . . . "

"I owe you one. Breakfast is served!"

I went behind the counter and realized I was smiling like an idiot. Olivier sat down on one of the stools.

"Coffee?"

"It seems it makes people happy . . . "

"It works with tea, too, you know."

"No, coffee will be perfect."

We took our time over breakfast, talking about the neighborhood, the rain, the good weather . . . it was nice. Olivier was really charming, and more than pleasant to look at with his lively brown eyes and dimples. I'd just learned that he was a physiotherapist when he looked at his watch.

"Damn! My first appointment."

"Oh . . . I'm so sorry; it's my fault."

"No, it's mine; it's nice here at your place. I think I'll be coming back often."

"The door will always be open to you . . . Go on now! Away with you!"

He rushed out.

Less than five minutes later, Felix showed up, a pathetic smile on his face.

"What a fraud! You arrive when the battle's over!"

"Well, I can see you've perked up after the battle! And besides, given what I know, you're not the one who worked up a sweat!"

My eyes opened wide and my mouth gaped open.

"How . . . how . . . do you . . . "

"The café across the street is awful, but it overlooked the love scene perfectly!"

"You planned all this."

"You couldn't miss seeing it all yesterday. That guy's hot for you; he's been hanging around the place for days. This morning was a test. He's a good guy; I can see you like him."

"No . . . not at all . . . "

"She's in love and stupid, adorable."

The first slap in the face of the day.

"He's nice, and there's nothing more to it than that. Get lost. And besides . . . he'll probably never set foot in here again."

"Tell me another!"

That evening, I was surprised to find myself watching people go up and down the street. I closed up without seeing Olivier again. I refused to admit I was disappointed. Nevertheless, I was enjoying my state of excitement: I felt alive, elated, delighted to be so light-hearted again during my daily routine. It was truly the first time I'd felt those emotions since Colin; the first time that a man aroused my interest and touched me by his simple presence.

Olivier was still going around and around in my head two days later. I was just closing up, turning over the sign on the door when he ran up to me. He leaned over and put his hands on his knees to catch his breath. I opened the door.

"Made it!" he said.

"We're closed!"

"I know, but you're still here. I missed you the last two days in a row, so I had to make it today."

"What do you want?"

"To take you out for a drink. You spend your evenings watching other people relax after a hard day's work. You have a right to relax, too . . . "

He must have seen how dumbfounded I looked.

"Unless someone is expecting you . . . I'm sorry, I should have thought of that . . . Fine . . . Umm . . . I'll get going . . . "

He turned and began walking away. I caught up with him in the street. I didn't want him to leave. Seeing him made me happy, that much was obvious.

"No one's expecting me."

"Really?"

"I'm saying it, so it's true!"

We walked back up the Rue Vieille-du-Temple to the Rue de Bretagne. We quickly found a table outside. Olivier asked me questions about Happy People, but I was evasive about how the café came about. He wanted to know who Felix was and what he meant to me. Given the expression on his face, I understood that my partner's homosexuality was very reassuring to him. I learned that he was thirty-seven and he'd studied in Belgium, where he'd had a practice for a long time before coming back to Paris a little over five years ago. "Back to my roots," he explained. I could see that the moment was coming when I'd have to tell him more about myself. So I decided to cut the evening short: I wasn't sure he was ready to hear who I really was and what I'd lived through. I felt good with him, and I panicked at the thought I might chase him away with all my baggage. Nevertheless, if something was going to happen between us, I couldn't hide my past from him. It was unimaginable. It was a real dilemma.

"Thanks for the drink, Olivier, but I've got to get home now. I've had a really nice time with you."

"The pleasure was all mine. Where do you live? Can I take you home?"

"That's kind, but I live above Happy People; you don't need to make sure I get home safely, I can manage."

"Will you let me walk part of the way with you?"

"If you'd like to . . . "

We set off. I felt uneasy, I couldn't manage to talk to him any more and didn't want to look at him. I felt embarrassed. Our walk lasted five minutes before Olivier decided to stop.

"I'll leave you here . . . "

I turned and looked at him. He found a way to smile at me again, even though I'd be silent for several minutes.

"Can I still come and see you at Happy People?" he asked.

"Whenever you like . . . see you soon."

I took two steps back without taking my eyes off of him, then turned around and headed for my apartment. In the pedestrian passage between the Rue Vieille-du-Temple and the Rue des Quatre-Fils, I glanced back over my shoulder: Olivier hadn't moved. He gave me a little wave. I sighed and continued on my way, smiling. I didn't know what to do any more . . . I went to bed as soon as I got home. It took a long time to fall asleep.

Felix didn't bring up how nervous I was the next few days, if he even noticed. I went about my business as usual, but I couldn't stop thinking about Olivier and a possible future romance. How could I tell him about my situation without sending him running? It was one thing to want to have a relationship and to feel ready for it, but quite another not to frighten someone away with my past and my fragility, the consequences of my previous life as a wife.

Saturday evening, calm. Glorious weather all day long, so my customers had deserted my bookstore to sit at outside cafés. I understood; I would have done the same. We were going to close early. I was behind the bar and Felix was sitting on a bar stool staring out into space.

"What have you got planned for tonight" I asked, pouring us each a glass of red wine.

"I can't decide; I'm in demand everywhere and I don't know whom I should honor with my presence."

I was so glad he was around: he always found a way to make me laugh.

"What about you?" he continued after we'd clinked glasses.

"Oh, I have a date with my television, *The Variety Show*."

"You haven't heard from your admirer?"

"No. I should have known I wouldn't. Besides, once he'd heard about Colin and Clara . . . and the rest, he'd run away so fast your head would spin."

"The rest? That foolish affair? That's ridiculous; some day that will be your downfall."

The very idea made me shake all over.

"No, I don't think so."

"Diane, you're jumping the gun. No one is asking you to get married again and start a family right away. You meet someone, have a good time with him, and see what happens."

"Anyway, it's a washout."

"Not so fast. Look who's coming . . . "

I looked up and saw Olivier, who was about to open the door. My heart started pounding.

"Hi," he said as he came inside.

"Hi, Olivier," Felix shouted with glee. "Have a seat!"

Felix patted the bar stool next to him, inviting him to sit down. Olivier walked cautiously forward, looking at my expression for permission.

"Will you have what we're having?" I asked.

"Why not!"

Felix took charge of the conversation, bombarding Olivier with questions about his life and work. Olivier willingly submitted to his interrogation. Using humor as a cover, my best friend was learning about the trustworthiness of this man; I knew him well enough to know that he would have sold his mother and father to find me someone, but the idea still terrified him. As for me, I didn't participate in their discussion; I couldn't have. So I washed all the dishes again. I cleaned each glass, each cup I found, several times in a row. I avoided looking at Olivier as soon as he tried to look at me. When I was forced to admit that there was nothing else to wash, rinse, polish . . . I picked up my packet of cigarettes from under the bar and went outside to get some air.

I was smoking my second ciggy when I heard the little bell: Felix.

"The King has chosen: I know where I'm headed to slum it."

"No . . . please . . . you can't leave me alone with him."

"His only fault is that he doesn't smoke. He's really a good guy. I can tell. Don't be crazy. Talk to him. Get out there. Enjoy life a little!"

He gave me a peck on the cheek.

"He's waiting for you."

Felix left, happy as a clam. I sighed deeply before going back inside.

"Well . . . " said Olivier.

"Well . . . "

"A quiet dinner for two: how does that sound?"

I went back behind the bar and took a sip of wine. Olivier didn't take his eyes off of me.

"Can we stay here?" I asked. "I'm closing and we can have the bar to ourselves for the evening."

"Would you let me get dinner?"

"Agreed!"

He jumped down from his bar stool and headed for the door, but hesitated and turned around to look at me.

"Will you still be here when I get back? You won't run away?"

"You can trust me."

He gave me a big smile and left.

To kill time before he came back, I shut the lights in the display windows and changed the sign—I was closed. I changed the music, put on the latest Angus & Julia Stone album and locked myself in the bathroom. I looked hideous; I'd been in a hurry that morning and didn't even have time to put on makeup. And I didn't smell fresh as a daisy, either. The problem was that I didn't want to risk Olivier finding the door locked when he came back and I didn't have enough time to go upstairs to my place. My cell phone vibrated in my pocket. Text message from Felix: "To fix up your face, look behind the photos next to the cash register." You'd think he had a hidden surveillance camera in the bathroom; anything was possible with him! Felix had actually stashed some makeup, a brush, and a sample of my perfume behind the counter.

I'd just finished setting the dishes on the counter when Olivier came back, his arms full of groceries.

"Did you invite your pals to join us?"

"I didn't know what to get," he replied, putting various bags down on the counter. "So I got everything. I went to the Greek place, the Italian shop, the cheese store . . . and then,

for dessert, I got some chocolate cakes, but then I wondered if
you might prefer fruit so I got some tarts . . . "

"You didn't have to do all that."

"I like doing things for you."

"Do you think I need someone to do things for me?"
He frowned.

"No . . . I find you attractive and I enjoy it . . . "

I looked at my feet, my legs shaking.

"It's not my place, but shall we sit down?"

He had the manners and skill to make me feel comfortable
and to ease the natural tension of this impromptu date.

I lost all sense of time. I couldn't remember having such an
enjoyable evening in years. Olivier made me laugh by telling
me stories about his patients and their imaginary back problems. I was starting to realize he was a spontaneous man with
no worries about the meaning of life, someone made happy
by the little things in life. He made it clear that he wanted to
know a little more about me.

"You always hold back a little . . . I wonder why . . . I don't
frighten you, do I?"

"No," I replied, smiling. "It's just that I haven't found myself in this situation for a long time . . . "

"Did you go through a bad break up? I'm sorry, that was a
little harsh . . . "

"No . . . It's more complicated than that . . . and it's not
easy to explain . . . "

"I don't want to force you to tell me . . . "

"But it's important . . . you might not want to see me again
afterward . . . "

"Only if you tell me you're a murderer . . ."

"I can assure you that I haven't killed anyone!" I replied, laughing.

I rolled my eyes and took a deep breath before starting.

"Actually, Olivier . . . I lost my husband and daughter in a car accident, three years ago . . ."

"Diane . . . I'm . . ."

"Don't say anything. That's enough for today. But there's been no one in my life since then . . . and I must say that . . . this is the first time I've had a nice time with a man. I'll understand if that frightens you . . ."

I hung my head in shame. I could see Oliver lean down to look into my eyes. I gave a little laugh. He hadn't closed up or seemed distant; he was the same.

"How about a little pick-me-up?"

"Sure."

"Can I go behind the bar to open another bottle?"

I nodded and watched him.

"You know this is a teenager's dream, don't you?" he added, laughing.

"Please, enjoy yourself!"

He found a bottle and corkscrew and poured us each a glass of wine. His concentration at carrying out his task was touching and relaxed me.

"You look good doing that. I could hire you."

"I only do special occasions," he replied, winking at me.

He was about to join me when he noticed the frame with all the family photos. He looked at me as if to ask permission.

"May I?"

"Go ahead."

He picked up the frame and studied it more closely.

"Felix looks like he was close to your daughter."

"He's her godfather . . . would you mind if I had a ciggy?"

"You're in your own place. Perhaps you don't want to talk about it?"

"If you have questions . . . " I replied, lighting my cigarette.

He put the pictures back where they belonged and came over to me.

"What have you been doing these past three years? I mean . . . to get through it . . . because no one could begin to imagine what you've lived through."

I breathed in deeply, took the time to finish and put out my cigarette before replying.

"I locked myself into our apartment . . . If I'm still alive, it's thanks to Felix. He shook me up so much that I decided to go away . . . I lived in Ireland for nearly a year, in a village in the middle of nowhere, with the sea a few meters from my doorstep . . . "

"What was it like?"

"Damp, but it revived me. It's beautiful, very, very beautiful, you know . . . the countryside is striking; it's a country worth seeing . . . "

I was fighting against my memories; I refused to allow myself to be haunted by the ghosts of Ireland.

"I ended up coming back to the fold, and I've been doing fine ever since. I don't want to die any more . . . I want to live, but a calm life, in Paris, at my bookstore. There you have it . . . "

I gave him a little smile.

"Thank you for having confided in me. I won't ask you about it anymore."

He gently pushed a lock of hair from my forehead and smiled. I shuddered.

"I'll help you clean up before letting you go home to bed."

He stood up and went behind the bar where he got started on the dishes. I joined him and dried the dishes he handed me. We were listening to "No Surprises," which played over and over again, without speaking. In the tiny space where we were, it was impossible not to brush against each other, touch each other's shoulders, and I liked that. When everything was clean and put away, Olivier put on his jacket.

"Do you go upstairs from in here?" he asked.

"Yes."

"Make sure everything's properly locked up."

I walked him to the door; we stood facing each other.

"Diane, I won't rush you; I'll give you time to come to me if you want to . . . I'll wait for you . . . as long as it takes . . . "

He came closer and whispered in my ear: "I'm not afraid."

Then he kissed me on the cheek. It wasn't the usual peck between friends that meant nothing—we'd never even done that. No, it was simply his lips against my cheek, and the proof of his promise of sensitivity.

"Good night."

"Thank you," I managed to whisper.

He went outside and waited until I'd locked the door before he walked away. I was in a daze, as if I was seeing everything through gauze cloth. I went upstairs and got into bed. Had I just found the man who would put joy in my life? Would I know how to let myself go?

4

Olivier came to see me almost every day for the next two weeks. Sometimes just to say hello, sometimes to stop for a coffee or a glass of wine in the evening after work. He never asked me to go out with him again, nor did he come near me. He let me get used to him being there; he was bringing me out of my shell and it was working. I watched the street more and more eagerly, hoping to see him coming; I was disappointed when he left and at night, when I went to bed, I was still thinking about him. And yet, I couldn't manage to take the step, to let him see how I felt. The idea of the future terrified me.

He'd spent his lunch break at Happy People and had just left when Felix attacked. I hadn't seen him coming.

"What are you playing at?"

"What?"

"That poor guy's starting to make me feel sorry for him. You're letting him stew while batting your eye lashes at him. You spend all day waiting for him to arrive and then you can barely speak, I can tell. What has to happen before you make a move?"

"I don't know . . ."

"Is it because of Colin? I thought you'd gotten past that."

"No, it's not Colin. To be honest, I think more about Olivier than him."

"That's a good sign."

"Yes . . . but . . ."

"Kindness and patience have their limits. Give him a little hope, otherwise . . ."

"Leave me the hell alone," I replied, frustrated by the truths he was forcing me to hear.

That very evening, Felix rolled his eyes at me when Olivier came in. He came over to me and smiled shyly.

"Are you free tomorrow evening?"

"Umm . . . yes . . ."

"Actually, I've invited some friends over who've been pestering me to have a housewarming party. I'd really like you to be there. And Felix, if you'd like to come, please do."

"We'll be there," I said, without giving Felix a chance to get a word in.

"I'll let you get back to work. Until tomorrow evening then!"

He waved at Felix. As he closed the door behind him, he looked back at me through the window. I smiled.

"See, it wasn't as complicated as all that!"

"Don't you dare embarrass me tomorrow night," I told Felix.

He burst out laughing.

When we rang Olivier's doorbell the next day, I was happy, absolutely stress free. In fact, I was eager to see him. I had decided to push my doubts and anxiety to the back of my mind. When Olivier opened the door, Felix, who was worse than a bull in a china shop, ditched us, giggling like a teenager.

"He'll make sure the party gets going, you know," I told Olivier.

"I hope he enjoys himself!"

We looked into each other's eyes.

"Thank you for inviting me tonight; I'm happy to be here with you."

And without thinking, I kissed him on the cheek.

"Will you introduce me?"

Olivier didn't need to make any introductions; all his friends had heard about me. He pretended to be embarrassed for their sake and winked at me. I was touched by their warm welcome; they did everything to make me feel I was one of them. Felix very quickly made himself at home, talking to everyone and telling jokes. Olivier poured me a glass of white wine and apologized for not being able to stay with me.

"I still have things to do in the kitchen."

I looked around at how he decorated his apartment. Nothing like a bachelor pad. Quite the contrary, it was a home. It was neither messy nor ridiculously minimalist. It was warm: the upholstery on the sofa made you want to curl up on it, the plants and photos of his family and friends brought everything to life and were welcoming. Everything reflected Olivier: comforting.

I laughed and talked to nice people of my own age; I felt I'd become a woman like any other again. I didn't cling onto Felix's coattails; I didn't feel threatened. I subtly reassured his curious friends: "Yes, I like Olivier! Give it time." They were a close-knit group of friends who honestly cared about each other's happiness. No one asked me about my private life; Olivier had been discreet.

My good mood collapsed like a house of cards when a woman came out of a room—that I assumed was Olivier's bedroom—with a six-month-old baby in her arms. She was glowing with happiness and maternal exhaustion. I wanted to scream and run like the wind; I stood away from the others, hoping she wouldn't see me. Naturally, she spotted me in a flash and came over to me with a big smile.

"Diane, is it? I'm so pleased to meet you. Olivier talks about you so much."

She gave me a peck on the cheek; I could smell the Mustela baby lotion, which took me back to when Clara was born. I'd always loved babies and the way they smelled. Colin often said: "You're sniffing your daughter!" Just before they died, we were thinking of having another baby to give Clara a little brother or sister . . .

"And this is the apple of my eye," she continued, showing me her baby. "I was giving her a bottle when you came in . . . Oh, damn, I left her cuddly toy in Olivier's bedroom! Can I leave her with you for a few seconds?"

Without waiting for my reply, she put her daughter in my arms. My head started pounding and ice ran through my veins. I no longer saw this little girl, I was seeing myself with *my* Clara in my arms. I could feel her skin, her tiny hand clutching my finger, her first little blond curls. Through this baby's gurgling, I could hear a silent scream run through my head. I started breathing more quickly. I was shaking so hard that I was going to drop her if I had to hold her for even one second longer. I was afraid that my pain might hurt her . . .

"Diane . . . Diane . . . "

I raised my eyes, full of tears, and saw it was Olivier who was calling me softly.

"I'll take her, OK?"

I nodded. Paralyzed, I watched Olivier take care of the little girl as if he had been doing it forever. He held her close, talked to her and handed her to the man I guessed was her father. Then he came back to me and put his arm around my waist.

"I need Diane in the kitchen!" he told the crowd.

Before we left the room, I caught sight of Felix, who looked upset. My friend was as white as a ghost. Olivier closed the door to his little kitchen, opened the window, took an ashtray out of the cupboard and handed me my pack of cigarettes that he must have grabbed on the way without me noticing. Shaking and in tears, I lit one. Olivier respected my silence.

"I'm so sorry," I said.

"Don't talk nonsense; no one noticed a thing. And even if they did, they won't say anything. Do you want me to get Felix?"

"No . . . "

I sniffled; he handed me a handkerchief.

"I'm not normal anymore . . . I can't . . . I can't see babies or children anymore . . . it hurts too much. Because each time, it reminds me that my daughter was taken away from me, my Clara, the love of my life . . . I'll never be able to accept that . . . I'll never be able to forget . . . to move on . . . "

I gasped. I would soon break down completely. Olivier came over to me, wiped my cheeks, and held me close. I immediately felt better; I was safe; I could feel how tender and gentle he was. He didn't take advantage of the situation. Little by little, my breathing returned to normal. I trusted him, but seeing him with that baby in his arms confirmed what I feared most within myself, the thing that prevented me from getting involved with him.

"I'm not the right woman for you . . . "

"Where did that come from?" he asked quietly.

I pulled away.

"If it works between us . . . "

He gently pulled me back into his arms and I let him.

"I have no doubts about that!" he said, stroking my cheek.

"I can never give you a child. I don't want to have any more . . . The mother I used to be died with Clara."

"Is that what's holding you back?"

"Some day, you're going to want to have a family. I saw you with that baby, you loved holding her. I'd feel bad about making you waste your time, you should find a woman who wants . . . "

"Shh!"

He placed his finger over my lips and looked into my eyes.

"I do like children, that's true, but I especially like them if they belong to someone else. It's not one of my goals in life. I believe that being a couple is enough in itself. And that's all I expect from a relationship between us, nothing more, I promise you. We have plenty of time to think about children . . . We could see how it goes and cross that bridge when we come to it, together," he said, smiling.

Life could be sweeter with a man like him by my side. His arms were strong and protective, his eyes lively, a soft hazel color, his face expressive. I only had to take the step. I slowly brought my face close to his and kissed him. He held me tighter; I opened my mouth slightly, put my arms around his neck, and we kissed even more deeply. Then Oliver pressed his forehead against mine. He stroked my cheek as I closed my eyes and smiled.

"I'd give anything to have everyone next door disappear," he said softly.

"So would I!"

"If it's too difficult, I'll take you home."

"No, I want to stay."

"I won't leave your side for a second, you can count on me."

We kissed again, intensely, for a long time. But we had to control ourselves. We stood a few inches apart, slightly breathless.

"Shall we go back in?" Olivier asked, frowning slightly.

"We don't have much choice."

We picked up the dinner plates from the counter—we had to keep busy. Before opening the door, Olivier kissed me one last time. Even though I tried, I couldn't avoid Felix's questioning looks: he saw that that I'd been crying, but that something else had happened as well. When he understood, his eyes opened wide and he gave me a lustful wink. I spent the rest of the evening at Olivier's side. I was quickly able to relax, for the baby had been put to bed, and didn't make a single sound. Whenever we felt that curiosity about us was aroused again, we always managed to brush it off. I was barely listening to the conversation; all I could think about was what had just happened, impatient to be alone with Olivier again.

Felix managed to corner me.

"Are you going to go home tonight?"

"I don't know, but don't wait for me if you want to leave."

"Hallelujah!"

Everyone left. Except me. As soon as we were alone, I crossed the room and kissed him again, pressing my body against his. My hands could finally explore his body; his hands were already stroking my back, sliding down to my waist.

"Can I stay tonight?" I whispered.

"Do you need to ask?" he replied.

Still holding onto him, I led us to his room, to his bed . . . I didn't feel raw passion when we made love; I needed tenderness, his touch, gentleness. Olivier was careful with each caress, each kiss. He was taking care of me; he didn't care about his pleasure, only mine. I knew I'd found the man I needed. A little later, falling asleep in his arms, I told myself I was no longer Colin's wife. I was just Diane.

In the month that followed, I rediscovered what life was like as a couple. We saw each other every day, except Sundays:

it was out of the question to give up my weekly brunch with Felix. I slept at his place regularly, but he didn't sleep at my place very often. I still found there were certain difficulties in revealing my innermost secrets. He wasn't demanding: he always let me come to him when I was ready.

It was summer. I'd told Olivier that I wasn't going to close. If he was disappointed that we wouldn't be going on vacation together, he didn't show it. One evening at the beginning of July, we were having a drink on the terrace when I suggested an alternative.

"Maybe we could go away for a long weekend?"

"I'd thought of that but wondered if you actually didn't want to go away with me," he replied, smiling slightly.

"Idiot!"

He laughed before continuing.

"Seriously, I know you don't want to go far from Happy People."

"You're right, it frightens me, but you're here now and we wouldn't be away for long. I hope that Felix can take care of everything . . ."

That night, Olivier slept at my place.

The long weekend of July 14 came just at the right moment. I was going to have to brief Felix and leave the bookstore for four days. Olivier had organized everything: destination, train tickets, hotel. But he thought I didn't give myself enough time off. Two days before we were leaving, he plotted with Felix so I could have an extra afternoon "as a test," they said, trying to justify themselves. To my great delight they got on like a house on fire; Olivier laughed at all of

Felix's outrageous behavior and was neither critical nor jealous of our intense, close friendship. As for Felix, he saw Olivier as Colin's successor; he appreciated his sense of humor and especially that he never asked indiscreet questions about the family I'd lost.

During the afternoon of the famous test, Olivier went with me to boutiques I hadn't been to in years; I took advantage of the sales to perk up my summer wardrobe. I followed him without thinking about where we were going; he led me through the streets of Paris, holding my hand. Suddenly, he stopped in front of a spa. I looked at him quizzically.

"A gift!"

"What?"

"For the next two hours, someone is going to pamper you. You're unwinding today before our vacation starts."

"You shouldn't have . . . "

"Shh! I enjoy doing it. Afterwards, go home, get ready, and I'll pick you up at 7 o'clock. I've found an exhibition you should like and we'll eat out afterwards."

I threw my arms around his neck. No one had thought of taking such good care of me since Colin.

I was relaxed, my skin was as soft as a baby's, and I'd slipped on a pretty black dress and platform sandals I'd bought that very afternoon. Before going down to the bookstore to wait for Olivier, I looked at myself in the mirror; I was happy to feel beautiful for him. Given the way he looked at me half an hour later, I wasn't disappointed.

In the metro, I hung onto him, gazed at him, and kissed his neck, as if I were a teenager in love. I'd turned the page on so many things. I couldn't imagine that anything could shatter the peaceful spell I'd lived under ever since Olivier came into my life. I was beginning to admit that I was in love with him. A sweet feeling ran through me.

We got out of the metro at Montparnasse. I followed Olivier without asking any questions. I was excited at the idea of going to an exhibition. He insisted on keeping it a surprise right until the last moment. When we got to our destination, he made me turn around with my back to the door, putting off the moment when I could discover where we were. I could hear music behind me: Celtic music in a Breton neighborhood, what could be more normal?

"I was leafing through the *Pariscope* listings when I came across this show. It isn't on for long, so we had to see it," said Olivier, pleased with himself.

"What's it about?"

"Come in and you'll see."

I pushed open the door. It was an exhibition about the relationship among British, Scottish, and Irish culture. They'd created a pub atmosphere; they didn't serve champagne and petit fours, just Guinness, whiskey, and vinegar-flavored potato chips. My excitement quickly fell and turned to terrible discomfort.

"You told me that Ireland had been good for you, so I thought you'd like this."

"Yes," I managed to say.

Olivier put his arm around my waist and we started to walk around the show. There were a great many people, so it was difficult to make our way through the crowd. I didn't dare look at any painting or photograph for fear of recognizing a landscape and feeling emotions surge through me. I responded to Olivier's questions in words of one syllable. I decided to accept his offer to have a Guinness.

"I have the impression this was a bad idea," he finally said.

"It's my fault; I told you that I'd loved Ireland, loved living next to the sea, and that's true . . . but I don't just have good memories; I wasn't in the best shape back then."

"Well, then, let's go. Seeing you suffer is the last thing I wanted. I'm really sorry."

"Don't blame yourself, but I would like to leave, I'm sorry. Let's continue our evening far away from all this."

We headed toward the door; I stood close to him, looking down at my feet. We were almost outside when a voice rang through the music and general brouhaha. A voice that stopped me in my tracks. A voice that took me back to Mulranny. A voice that left the taste of the sea spray on my lips. A hoarse voice that had the odor of tobacco and that I never thought I'd hear again.

"Wait here," I said to Olivier, breaking free of him.

I left him standing there and retraced my steps, guided and hypnotized by the echo of that voice; it resonated like the song of the Sirens. It wasn't possible. I was imagining it, disoriented by the wave of memories that flooded through me in this place. Yet I should have felt nothing. I looked at people's shapes, their faces, listened to their conversations, pushed aside anyone who got in my way. And then I froze. It definitely was his voice. We were standing only a few inches apart. He was here: standing with his back to me, tall, scruffy, wearing a shirt and no jacket, a cigarette in his hand waiting to be lit. If I breathed in, his scent would waft through me and send me back into his arms. I was shaking, my mouth was dry, my hands damp, I was hot and cold both at the same time.

"Edward . . . " I whispered; I couldn't stop myself.

I had the impression that everyone had heard me. He alone counted. His body tensed, he lowered his head for a few seconds, tightened his fists, and clicked his cigarette lighter nervously several times in a row. Then he turned around. We stood staring at each other. My eyes were full of questions and surprise. After looking me up and down, his expression was cold, distant. His features were still as harsh and arrogant as ever, hidden by his beard. His hair was still as messy as I remembered but now showing a little grey. He looked exhausted, marked by something I couldn't manage to define.

"Diane," he said at last.

"What are you doing here?" I asked, my voice trembling, naturally switching back into English.

"I'm exhibiting my photographs."

"How long have you been in Paris?"

"Three days."

His reply hit me like a blow to the heart.

"Were you going to come to see me? . . ."

"No."

"Oh . . ."

So many questions were going through my mind but I couldn't ask a single one. His distant, hostile attitude froze me to the spot. He looked behind me and I felt a hand on my back.

"I was looking for you," said Olivier.

How could I have forgotten him? I forced myself to smile and turned towards him.

"Forgive me . . . I . . . I noticed Edward as we were leaving and . . ."

He held out his hand.

"Enchanté, I'm Olivier."

Edward shook his hand without saying a word.

"Edward doesn't speak French," I said.

"Oh, I'm sorry! I didn't think you'd run into anyone you knew here," he said in perfect English, smiling.

"Edward's a photographer and . . ."

"I lived next door to Diane when she was in Mulranny."

That's not how I would have described it. It had been much more than that. And my pounding heart was sending me contradictory signals about what he still meant to me.

"Amazing! And you meet again here; what an incredible coincidence. If I'd known . . . Diane, do you want to stay now? You have to make up for lost time; you surely have things to tell each other . . ."

"No," Edward interrupted. "I have work to do. Delighted to have met you, Olivier."

Then he looked at me.

"Take care of yourself."

I panicked when I saw him about to walk away from me.

"Wait!"

I caught him by the arm. He stared at my hand on him. I quickly let go.

"How long will you be here?"

"I'm flying back tomorrow night."

"Oh . . . you're leaving already? . . . Could you spare a little time for me?"

He wiped his hand down his face.

"I don't know."

"Please, come to the bookstore. Please . . . "

"I don't see what good that will do," he muttered.

"We obviously have things to say to each other."

He held his burnt-out cigarette in the corner of this mouth and stared into my eyes.

"I can't promise."

I rifled through my bag for a business card from Happy People.

"The address and a map are on the back. Call me if you can't find it."

"I'll find it."

He glanced at me one last time, nodded at Olivier, turned and walked quickly away.

"Shall we go?" asked Olivier. "Are we still going to the restaurant?"

"Yes, of course. Nothing's changed."

Before going out the door, I turned around. Edward was talking to various people while staring at me the whole time.

Half an hour later, we were sitting in an Indian restaurant. Every bite was torture, but I forced myself for Olivier. His kindness and attention never faltered in spite of what I'd just done to him. He didn't deserve this. I couldn't leave him in the dark any longer. But I'd have to be cautious about what I said.

"I'm sorry about what just happened," I began. "I shouldn't have left you alone like that . . . but it was so strange to see someone I knew . . . I spoiled your surprise."

"Not at all. You're shaken up and I don't like seeing you like this."

"I'll be fine, don't worry. Being back in an Irish atmosphere sent me back to a period in my life that was very confusing."

"And Edward? Who is he?"

His tone of voice had no suspicion whatsoever.

"He was my neighbor, as he said. I rented the cottage next to his and my landlords were his aunt and uncle, Abby and Jack. Wonderful people . . . I was friends with his sister Judith, a heterosexual version of Felix."

"That must be something!"

"She's amazing."

"And since you left?"

"I left Ireland on a whim, hurriedly said my goodbyes and never contacted anyone. Now I'm ashamed of how selfish I was."

"You shouldn't be," he said, taking my hand, "They could have gotten in touch with you."

"They're not the kind of people to get involved in other people's lives; they always respected my silence. Nothing changed when I left."

"Is that why you wanted to see him tomorrow?"

"Yes . . . "

"He's not very talkative; do you think you'll get anything out of him?'

I couldn't help but laugh at his remark.

"He won't say much, just what's strictly necessary, but that's always better than nothing."

I sighed and stared at my empty plate.

"Do you want to be alone tonight?"

He looked into my eyes.

"No. Let's go to your place."

Once we went to bed, Olivier didn't try to make love to me; he kissed me and simply held me in his arms. He fell asleep fairly quickly, but I never closed my eyes at all that night. I was reliving every detail of my unexpected encounter. Only a few hours ago, Ireland was a finished chapter in my life, a closed book, and it had to remain that way. If he did come the next day, I'd ask how everyone was, he'd go away again, and I'd get on with my life.

Despite being very careful, I woke Olivier when I got out of bed.

"Are you feeling better?" he asked, sounding sleepy.

"Yes. Go back to sleep. Enjoy your vacation."

I kissed him.

"I'll come and see you after work."

I kissed him again and left.

Forty-five minutes later, I opened the bookstore without having eaten my usual croissant. My stomach was in knots. My regular morning clients must have sensed I was in a bad mood; they left me alone to think in my corner. When I saw

Felix coming in around noon, I knew there was going to be a scene. If Edward did actually come, Felix would have a front row seat. And how could I forget that the last time they saw each other they'd had a fistfight!

"You've got one of those bad expressions on your face today! What happened? Did Olivier run out of steam?"

He was on the attack. I was going to reply just as aggressively.

"Edward is in Paris. I ran into him last night."

He collapsed onto the nearest barstool.

"I must still be hallucinating from the X!"

Completely unwillingly, I burst out laughing.

"No, Felix. It's the absolute truth, and he might be stopping by today."

Seeing the look on my face, he realized it wasn't a joke. He stood up, came behind the bar and took me in his arms.

"Are you OK?"

"I don't know."

"What about Olivier?"

"I didn't tell him what happened between us."

"Did he come because of you?"

"Not really, judging from the greeting I got . . . He's exhibiting his photographs and going back tonight."

"Good. Well, it could have been worse. I'm going to work a full day today. Just so I can watch what happens!"

I burst out laughing.

It was the longest day I ever worked. All I did was wait. Felix watched me out of the corner of his eye and played the fool to relax me. The longer the day dragged on, the more convinced I was that he wouldn't come. Which, in truth, wouldn't be so bad. It was dangerous to stir things up again.

I was handing change to a customer when he showed up, a backpack slung over his shoulder. My bookstore suddenly seemed very small; Edward took up the whole room. He shook hands with Felix—who had the good sense not to make any sarcastic joke—sat down at the bar, and observed my world with the greatest attention. Several long minutes passed. His bluish-green eyes took in the books, the glasses, and the photos on the counter. He finally stared straight into my eyes, without saying a word. So many feelings rose to the surface: our fights, the few kisses we shared, my decision, his admission of how he felt, our separation. The tension must have been unbearable to Felix, for he was the first to speak.

"A glass of beer, Edward?"

"Don't you have anything stronger?" he replied.

"How about a ten-year-old scotch?"

"Neat."

"Coffee, Diane?"

"That would be great. Thanks, Felix. Could you take care of the customers, if there are any?"

"That's what I'm paid for!" he replied, winking at me as encouragement.

Edward thanked Felix and knocked back his whiskey. I understood him well enough to know that he could sit there for an hour without saying a word unless I started the conversation. After all, I was the one who'd asked him to come.

"So, you have a show in Paris, just like that?"

"It seemed like a good opportunity."

He rubbed his weary eyes. Why did he look so tired?

"How are you?"

"I'm working a lot. And you?"

"I'm fine."

"Good for you."

What else could I tell him about myself? And how could I get him to talk?

"And Judith? What's she been up to?"

"Still the same."

"Is there a man in her life?"

He had to react to such a question.

"Several," he said, sighing.

Bad choice of question.

"And how are Abby and Jack? Are they well?"

I was sure not to put my foot in my mouth asking about them. But for the first time, he wouldn't look at me. He stroked his beard, got somewhat agitated, and took his cigarettes out of his pocket.

"What's going on, Edward?"

"Jack's fine . . . "

"And Abby?"

"I'll be right back."

He went outside and lit a cigarette. I grabbed one too and joined him.

"You didn't stop either, I see," he said, mockingly.

"No reason to . . . but we weren't discussing our mutual smoking habit."

I stood right in front of him.

"Edward, look at me."

He did. I understood that what I was about to hear wasn't going to be pleasant.

"Abby? She's fine, isn't she?"

It was unimaginable to think the contrary; I could picture her on her bike the first day I met her, so lively in spite of her age.

"She's sick."

"But . . . she's going to get better?"

"No."

My hand flew up to cover my mouth. Abby was the heart, the rock of that family, so maternal, so kind, so generous. I remember when she thought I was too thin and practically force-fed me slice after slice of carrot cake. I could still feel her final hug when I said goodbye to her, and how she'd replied "Do keep in touch." Even though I didn't realize it at the time, Abby had been a strong influence on my start through the healing process, and I had pushed her away.

I was trying to compose myself when I realized that Olivier was standing next to us. Edward saw that I hadn't noticed him and turned around. They shook hands and Olivier gave me a discreet little kiss on the lips.

"Are you all right?" he asked.

"Not really. Edward just gave me some very bad news. Abby is not well at all."

"I'm terribly sorry," he said to Edward. "I'll leave you alone then, it will be easier to talk that way."

He stroked my cheek, went inside the bookstore, and joined Felix. I watched him go, then turned toward Edward who was staring hard at me. My stomach was in knots, I looked up toward the heavens, breathing hard before being able to speak to him again.

"Tell me more, please . . . "

He shook his head and remained silent.

"It isn't possible . . . I can't believe what you've just . . . "

"She'll be happy to know you're well. She never stopped worrying about you."

"I want to do something . . . Can I get in touch with her?"

He gave me a gloomy look.

"I'll tell her that I saw you; that will be enough."

He looked at his watch.

"I have to go."

He opened the door long enough to pick up his backpack and wave goodbye to Felix and Olivier. When he came back, I said.

"I have a question to ask you before you leave."

"I'm listening."

"It has nothing to do with Abby, but I need to know. I tried to call you, twice, a few months ago. I even left a message. Did you get it?"

He lit another cigarette and looked straight into my eyes.

"Yes."

"Why didn't you . . . "

"Diane, there's been no room for you in my life for a long time now . . . "

He gave me less than five seconds to take in the blow.

"Olivier seems like a good person. It was right for you to rebuild your life."

"I don't know what to say."

"Then don't say anything."

I took a step towards him but stopped myself at the last minute.

"Goodbye, Diane."

He turned and walked away without giving me a chance to reply. I didn't take my eyes off of him until he disappeared at the end of the street. I was fighting back the tears. My memories of utopia were shattered. When I thought of Mulranny, nothing ever changed: Abby was happy, Jack strong, Edward alone, with his dog and his photos. How could I have imagined that life wouldn't go on without me? Was I really so self-centered? But life with Abby sick and dying was unacceptable. I wanted to cry for her, her pain, her loss, for Edward, who wasn't really the same now, because I realized that my Ireland didn't exist anymore. It was almost as if, up until now, I had subconsciously lived in the hope that we would all meet again, share good news . . .

It was over. I had Olivier now, and Edward had a woman in his life. Each of us had turned the page. But Abby . . . how could I not think about her?

5

Our romantic long weekend away came just at the right moment. Without knowing it, Olivier had made the right decision in deciding to take me to the Mediterranean coast; the sun, warmth, lyrical voices, cool morning dew, and my bathing suit would put everything back into proper perspective.

Those four days were a wonderful escape, and I couldn't help but grow closer to him. He anticipated all my desires; every one of his actions, his gestures, was gentle; every word he spoke considerate. He wanted me to relax and rest, so much so that we refused to rush around exploring the area. I rediscovered the meaning of the word "vacation," thanks to long naps I allowed myself to take, and swimming and eating out in restaurants in the evening. We took our time doing nothing, together, and it was good. I almost forgot about the bookstore.

We were leaving the next day. We were having lunch on the terrace when my mind wandered and I wondered if Felix was managing.

"What are thinking about, Diane?"

"Felix," I replied, laughing.

"Are you worried?"

"A little . . . "

"Call him."

"No. I can wait another twenty-four hours."

"You already deserve a medal for not thinking about it until now! I was really expecting it much sooner. Don't hesitate because of me."

"Thanks! I'll call him from the beach; that will make him furious!"

Olivier burst out laughing.

"I didn't realize you were a sadist."

"He loves it; there's nothing I can do about it . . . Let's have another drink!"

An hour later, I was basking in the sun while Olivier had a swim. Like the two days before, he'd made sure to find us a little spot where children couldn't climb on the rocks, so I wasn't in danger of getting upset. I could feel my body warming up again, and I liked it, especially the suntan that made my skin glisten; that hadn't happened since my last family vacation. And one thing made me particularly happy: the complete absence of guilt. Time to celebrate!

"Happy People does fuck-all in July, how can I help you?"

It had been a very long time since I didn't care about what was happening at Happy People.

"Felix, you should see me! I'm as brown as a berry, slightly tipsy thanks to a nicely chilled bottle of Côtes-de-Provence, and I'm about to join my lover for a swim."

"Who is this strange woman I'm talking to?"

"Your one and only, your boss!"

"So just like that, you start laughing like a madwoman?"

"Yes. And how are you? Is the bookstore still there?"

"I managed to avoid fires, floods, and burglaries, so you could say I'm managing."

"So all in all, it's time I got home. I'll be inspecting the premises as soon as I'm back tomorrow night."

"It's good to hear you sounding the way you do. Enjoy every minute you've got left."

"That's just what I intend to do."

"I was afraid you'd go back into your shell that after that other guy showed up, and especially after hearing about Abby."

"Everything's fine. Olivier's waving to me so I'll have to go now."

I hung up and stuffed my phone into my bag. I fought holding it against Felix for making that last remark. I'd worked hard to put Abby out of my mind and to enjoy Olivier. I had to keep going. I breathed in deeply, took off my sunglasses, and headed for the water. I swam out to him and clung onto his shoulders, my arms around his neck. He smiled and kissed my arm.

"Is everything all right?"

"Let's not talk about Paris."

Our last night in the hotel. We'd just made love, tenderly,

as always, and I felt afraid. Afraid of losing something after this little vacation, quite simply, fear of losing this feeling of peace. Olivier was spooning me, holding me tight. I absent-mindedly stroked his arm while looking out of the window we'd left open.

"Diane, you've been distracted for several hours . . . "

"No I haven't."

"Is there a problem with the bookstore, or Felix?"

"Absolutely not."

"Tell me what's worrying you."

I wanted him to stop! Be quiet! Why was he so considerate, so perceptive? I didn't want him to be the one to burst our bubble.

"It's nothing, I promise."

He sighed and kissed my neck.

"You're a terrible liar. You're worried about the woman who was your landlady in Ireland, aren't you?"

"You're getting to know me very well . . . it's true, I am thinking about her and I just can't believe it. I'm only starting to realize now how much she did to help me . . . And to think she's going to . . . No, it isn't possible. I want to do something, but what?"

"Start by calling her. That would be a good first step."

"I don't know if I can."

"It will take courage, but you're stronger than you think. When I met you, I could sense how fragile you were, but you're actually strong, unbelievably strong. You'll manage."

"I'll think about it."

I turned over and kissed him. I needed to feel his body

next to mine, to cling on to him. I refused to think about the possible consequences of that phone call.

It took me a month to make the decision and find the right time to do it. I was never alone. At the bookstore, Felix was always hanging around; the rest of the time I was with Olivier, and I couldn't imagine calling Abby with him standing next to me. To tell the truth, I was putting it off because I was so afraid of what I might find out. I took advantage of Felix being away on vacation at the end of August to build up the courage.

"Hello?"

Even though her voice sounded a bit tired, I recognized Abby, which made it impossible for me to say a word.

"Hello! . . . Who is it?"

"Abby . . . It's me . . . "

"Diane? Is it really you?"

"Yes. Forgive me for not having . . . "

"Hush, my darling. I'm so happy to hear your voice. When Edward told us he'd seen you . . . "

"So he told you?"

"Happy again! He told us you were fine and that you'd met someone! That's wonderful!"

That made things clear.

"Thank you . . . And what about you? How are you?"

"Absolutely fine!"

"Abby," I scolded, "He didn't go into detail, but Edward said . . . "

"He deserved to be told off for that; he shouldn't have worried you . . . "

It was as if I'd only left her yesterday.

"No, he was right. What's going on with you?"

"Well, you know, I'm a tired old lady with a weak heart . . ."

"You're not old!"

"You're sweet, Diane. Don't be upset. That's life . . . It's good to hear your voice; I miss you a lot."

"I miss you too, Abby."

"Oh, if I gave in to myself, I'd ask you to do something for me."

"Anything you want!"

"Come and see us."

Go back to Ireland, to Mulranny . . . It had never crossed my mind.

"Oh . . . I don't know . . . "

"I'd so love to have everyone with me once again. And Judith would be mad with joy. You're her only real friend."

Abby knew how to play on people's feelings when it suited her . . . I should have remembered that! The bell on the front door tinkled: Olivier was coming to help me close up.

"I can't promise but I'll see what I can do."

"Don't leave it too long, my darling."

"Don't say that."

I glanced over at Olivier who had understood who I was talking to and gave me a sweet smile.

"I'll . . . I'll call you back soon."

"Thank you for calling, Diane. See you soon. Lots of love."

"You too, Abby, you too."

I put my phone down on the counter and fell into Olivier's

arms. One more minute and I'd be crying. I already wanted to be there with her, in her living room, by the fireplace, telling her over and over again that she was going to get better. How could I just suddenly leave for Ireland? What about the bookstore? Olivier? Felix?

"Was it as bad as that?"

"She's talking as if she's already gone."

"I'm so sorry, Diane . . . "

"I'm going to have to refuse to do the favor she asked."

"What's that?"

"Let's close up and I'll tell you about it later."

"If that's what you want."

I needed to take it all in before explaining everything to him. The bookstore was all locked up in less time than I needed to say everything. Olivier went out to get us some falafel for dinner. While we were eating, I managed to tell him what Abby had asked, the thing I couldn't stop thinking about.

"Are you afraid it will be too difficult for you?"

"No, I'm not thinking about me; it's Abby I'm worried about."

"So why don't you want to go?"

"The bookstore . . . "

"Felix managed very well when we went away."

I refused to believe it might be possible.

"What about you? I won't leave you . . . Would you like to come with me?"

"No, Diane. For several reasons. I can't take any more vacation days, and even if I could, they're your friends; I wouldn't want to prevent you from having a good time with them by tagging along. It's not my place. And I could help Felix, if that would make you feel better."

I was so terrified by what was happening that I let out a great sigh. He put his hands around my face and looked into my eyes.

"The only thing I'd ask of you is to be sure. Do you want to go back to Ireland? Do you feel you need to go?"

"Yes." I had to admit it.

For the first time, I took advantage of the Wi-Fi in the bookstore and reserved a flight and rental car while I was working. Abby absolutely refused to let me stay in a hotel: I'd stay with them. I warned Felix I'd be away by text, without admitting where I was going. As much as Olivier respected my decision, it would be a very different matter with my best friend. But I had no time to lose.

My flight to Dublin was three days after he got back from vacation.

The morning he came back to work, I was as tense as could be. I let him tell me all about his vacation before dropping the bomb. He was ahead of me.

"So, you two are so much in love that you want to go away again and lock yourself in a hotel room for several days? Tell all!"

"Actually . . . I'm not going away with Olivier."

"Oh, really! So what are you doing?"

"I'm going to see Abby."

"What? Are you kidding?"

"No."

"Are you completely crazy?"

"I'm not asking for your approval. I asked Olivier to come with me, you know, and he said no."

"If he knew what you'd gotten up to with Edward, he'd go! He's playing with fire. I thought he was more intelligent than that."

"You're wrong."

Felix gave me the cold shoulder right until I left. Yet, when I was saying goodbye to him, I could feel all his anxiety.

"Do you love Olivier? I mean, really love him?"

"I think so, yes . . . at least, I'm in love with him . . . "

"Have you told him?"

"No, not yet."

"In that case, be careful in Ireland."

"Felix, I'm coming back in less than a week; I don't see what could happen to me."

Olivier took me to the airport, even though I told him it wasn't necessary. And I knew he'd be there to meet me when I got back. He spared me advice about being careful. I was depressed at the idea of not seeing him for a week—proof that Felix was wrong. I let him hold me until the last minute.

"I'll call you very soon," I said, in between kisses.

"Everything will be fine, I'm sure of it."

I kissed him one last time and headed for the departure gate.

It was strange. As soon as I set foot in Ireland again, I felt like I was home, as if I were going back home after a long absence. I wasn't prepared to feel so good. I thought I'd feel bad, sad, in anguish, haunted by memories. But it was just the opposite. Every step, every kilometer I drove was natural, bringing me closer to home. My body and mind had held on to a clear memory of this journey.

As I approached Mulranny, I slowed down. One last hill and the bay appeared. I was so moved by the sight that I stopped on the side of the road. A gust of wind messed my hair up as soon as I opened the car door; I burst out laughing. I stood dead still, admiring the landscape that had been my whole world for so many months. My God! How I'd missed it! I could make out my cottage in the distance, and Edward's. I was shivering, looking at the sky and taking deep breaths of the clean, salty air. My eyes started to tear from the wind, and I liked those tears; it was as if they were cleansing my eyes and my cheeks. The dark days were behind me; all I thought about were the magical moments spent in this place. This trip was my opportunity to make peace with that period of my life.

When I arrived in the village, I was struck by how nothing had changed. Everything was as I remembered: the grocery store, the gas station, and the pub. I was seconds away from stopping to do some shopping and make a detour to the pub to drink some Guinness. On the other hand, it seemed too soon to go to the beach; I had plenty of time to do that. I immediately headed for Abby and Jack's place. I hadn't even turned off the engine when the door opened and I saw them standing there. I was smiling, laughing, and crying all at once. I ran toward them so Abby wouldn't get tired. Jack came on ahead of her and, to my great surprise, took me in his enormous arms.

"Our little Frenchwoman is finally here!"

"Jack . . . thank you."

"I'm the one who's dying," said Abby, "hand her over!"

Jack's expression warned me not to react to his wife's sense of humor. He let go of me and I got closer to her. She was smaller than I remembered and she'd lost weight. I guessed she'd done everything she could to hide the marks of her illness: foundation, concealer, and blusher. Her eyes were still mischievous and full of life. She took me in her arms and hugged me.

"It's so nice to have you here! I've been waiting for you to come back for more than a year."

I stopped myself from replying, "Me too."

An hour later, after unpacking my suitcase and sorting out my things in the dresser of my room, I was in the kitchen with her, preparing dinner. That was when I noticed the first signs of her weariness, for a year ago, she would have refused to let me help. Jack went from the kitchen to the living room, a Guinness in hand. Abby sat on a chair and bombarded me with questions about my life in Paris, Felix, whom she remembered fondly, and Olivier. I still couldn't believe that Edward told her about him: he really had changed! I let my curiosity get the better of me.

"So does he have someone in his life?"

Abby gave me a little smile.

"Yes . . . someone who takes up a lot of his time."

A wave of panic rushed through me.

"Abby, don't tell me that it's . . . "

Her laughter made me stop.

"She never came back, that one. Don't worry . . . the arrival of this other person has been a joy in our lives, you'll see. You're bound to meet up."

Thank you, God! Fortunately, I had Olivier, because if I'd still been on my own, it would have been difficult for me to bear seeing Edward with someone else, especially if she was someone really nice, as they were saying, and whom everyone liked.

During dinner, I caught up on what had been happening to the people who lived there whom I remembered. And, to tell the truth, I remembered everyone. Abby told me that Judith was coming for the weekend and that she was really well. I was going to have to face a difficult fifteen minutes when she demands an update on my love life! I started clearing up and forbid them to do a thing. I wanted them to rest while I was staying with them; it was the least I could do. I was familiar with everything in the house, a little as if I was at my grandparents' place where I'd spent all my vacations as a child. When everything was done, I went outside to smoke a cigarette, sitting on the front steps. I could hear the sea and the waves in the distance. I breathed in deeply, so relaxed that my body was like rubber. Jack joined me a few minutes later, with his cigar.

"Abby went upstairs to bed," he told me.

"I hope I'm not tiring her out too much."

"With everything you're doing, I wouldn't worry about that! You couldn't have given her a better present. She had a hard time getting over it when you left."

"I'm so sorry . . ."

"Don't be, that's what she's like; she wants to keep everyone close, forever, as if you were children. I just hope you didn't force yourself to come because of her."

"Not at all . . . I had a few concerns, I'll admit . . . but since I got here I know that it's the best decision I ever made."

I was nice and warm under the duvet in my enormous special bed. I'd just hung up with Olivier; it had done me good to talk to him and to be in contact with my life in Paris. I was much more attached to this place than I cared to admit. I was about to turn out the bedside lamp when I heard someone knocking at my door. I was stunned to see Abby there, wearing her bathrobe.

"I thought you were asleep . . . "

"I have trouble sleeping . . . and I wanted to know if you were comfortable."

"You'd have to be very choosy not to be."

She came over to the bed, sat down next to me and took my hands in hers.

"You look radiant, Diane."

"Thank you."

"We're going to make up for lost time."

"Yes."

"If you only knew how happy I am to have you here for a few days . . . My other daughter is home . . . "

I was too moved to speak.

"Go to sleep now."

She stood up and I stretched out. She leaned over and kissed my forehead.

"Sleep tight, my little one."

I fell into a peaceful sleep.

The next afternoon, Abby wanted us to go for a walk together on the beach. Jack dropped us off in the car not too far away, so she wouldn't get too tired. We walked along slowly, arm in arm. Abby's hand calmed my shaking; all I could see was my cottage. I had thought I would die of sadness in that house. But its four walls had also helped me become the person I was today.

"No one's lived there since you left."

"Why?"

"Because it's yours . . . I've brought the keys; do you want to go in?"

"No, I don't want to stir up all those memories."

"I understand."

We continued strolling down the beach, but not without feeling a few drops of rain. But I trusted Jack's sixth sense when it came to the weather, and he'd assured us there wouldn't be a heavy shower for several hours. I loved this beach, the sea that was so blue and slightly menacing, the wind that hardly ever died down. I'd mourned Colin and Clara in this place, I'd laughed, gotten to know the real Edward, met Judith. And I'd rolled around in the sand.

"Does Edward still have his dog?"

"He's madder than ever! Look, here he comes now."

Abby let go of me and stepped back a little, laughing. Hearing his barking filled me with joy and excitement. I'd spent a lot of time with Postman Pat! He ran toward us. I slapped my knees to get him to come to me, and, just like before, he jumped up and knocked me down.

"How are you, my little doggie?" I asked, as he licked my face.

"He recognizes you," said Abby.

"It's unbelievable!"

I managed to get up and throw a stick for him far into the distance, wondering where his master was.

"Does Edward let him out alone now?"

"No. He must be with Declan."

"Who's Declan?"

Before Abby could answer me, a little voice called at the top of its lungs from behind her. I turned around and leapt back when I saw a little boy running towards us, or rather, towards Abby. He threw his arms around her and nestled his head against her stomach. A knot formed in my throat; the presence of this child was ruining my homecoming on this beach and brought up too many questions for my peace of mind.

"Abby!"

"Yes, Diane?"

"Whose child is this?"

She looked uncomfortable, which rarely happened, and that added to my anguish.

"Well, whose is he?"

"He's mine," said Edward, from behind me.

I immediately turned around. He was less than a few feet away from me, and was staring straight into my eyes, the resemblance was striking. This little boy, whom you could tell would grow up to be a sturdy young man, was like a mini Edward: messy blond hair, proud, chiseled features, but with a smile as well. But this child was at least five years old . . .

Doing the math was interrupted by a little hand pulling at my coat.

"What's your name?"

Stunned speechless, I stared at him; the same disturbing eyes as his . . .

"Declan, I want you to meet Diane; she's a friend of the family," Abby replied. "We're going to let daddy talk to her, all right?"

He gave a little shrug.

"Edward, both of you come and have dinner at the house," Abby suggested. "I'll take Declan with me."

"It's out of the question that you walk back; I'll give you a lift."

"I don't think that your son needs to hear your conversation with Diane."

"I'll drop you off and come back and meet Diane afterwards."

My opinion obviously didn't count. Just like old times! Edward whistled for his dog, gestured to his son to follow him without saying a word, and headed for the car parked in front of his house. Abby came over to me.

"Can you help me walk?" she asked, taking my arm.

But I was the one clinging on to her, not the other way around. I stared at my feet, incapable of looking straight ahead at such a domestic scene: Edward walking with his son and his dog.

"Don't be too hard on him, my darling," she said to me before getting in the car.

Edward came over; I stepped back and glared at him.

"Do you want to wait at my place?"

"And then what?"

"Don't start . . . "

I recognized his curt tone of voice. I was losing my temper but stopped myself out of respect for Abby. I turned away and headed for the beach.

For a quarter of an hour, I paced back and forth, threw stones into the water with all my might, and chain-smoked cigarettes. So now he was a father! If there was one thing in the world that was impossible, it was that. If he had gone back to some woman, that would have been completely normal; she might have even already had children. But for him to have a son of his own, and one he couldn't deny was his! And a child of that age as well! Why did he always have to try me?

The screeching of his tires told me he was back. I stiffened even more and shouted as soon as he came over to me.

"How could you have hidden such a thing from me? You have a son who's more than five years old! And you told me nothing? Is that your philosophy, to lie and hide whatever is most important in your life? You'd already hidden your slut from me! And now, your . . . "

"Be quiet! What right do you have to ask me questions? You left! You never tried to find out how we were! You rebuilt your life!"

His attack stopped me in my tracks. He turned away and lit a cigarette. I felt terrible; the time for reproaches had come. He was right. I'd left him just at the point when he was ready to do so many things with me. But I couldn't stop myself; I needed answers.

"Did you know about him when I was here?"

"How could you think such a horrible thing?" he retorted, turning to face me again, a dark look in his eyes.

"Don't think you can get off so easily. I'm not going to wait for Judith to arrive to find out what's been happening in your life. That time is long gone. Either you explain where he came from right now . . . "

"Or what?"

"Or I leave. Tonight."

I didn't like what I was doing but I didn't have a choice. He said nothing.

"If I leave now, Abby's the one who will suffer."

He ran his hands through his hair and looked at the sea.

"I found out about Declan just over six months ago. And he's been living here for four months."

He walked towards the rocks and sat down on one. I watched him for a long time before deciding to join him. He looked so awful; I watched him smoke his cigarette in his unique way. If he could have swallowed it whole, he would have. The weariness I'd noticed when I saw him in Paris was palpable. It was more than that: it was exhaustion, physical exhaustion. He was crushed by a weight that he couldn't seem to lift. Things had changed between us, but his distress was unbearable to me, and what I was asking him to do by confiding in me was difficult for him. He glanced at me sideways when I sat down next to him. I pulled the collar of my jacket up and waited for him to continue.

"Judith must have told you that after I broke up with Megan, I went away to the Aran Islands by myself, right?"

"Yes."

"What she never knew was that I made a stop in Galway before getting the boat. I got drunk to forget. From the first night, I was with a woman who was also drinking to escape something, I never knew what. You can easily imagine how that ended up . . . It lasted three days . . . We only got out of bed to get our alcohol levels back up. One morning, when I woke up, I remembered that I'd left the dog in my car. The poor thing . . . I realized what I was turning into: a guy who drinks and sleeps with anyone to get back at his ex . . . I was pathetic; it wasn't like me. I left on the boat without saying goodbye; I cut myself off from everyone for two months on the Aran Islands and forgot about the girl. I could barely remember her name. Except she never had the chance to forget me."

He stopped talking to light a cigarette. He'd been left feeling less self-confident due to his sense of responsibility.

"Are you living together?"

He smiled at me, sadly.

"She's dead."

Ice ran through my veins. I felt bad for his little boy.

"How did you know he was your son? How old is he?"

"He's six . . . After you left, I worked hard to . . . Anyway, my name started to be heard in a lot of places. I was asked to cover a regatta in Galway. One day, when I got off the boat, she was waiting for me at the port. She'd been trying to find me for months. It took me ages to recognize her, not because of my foggy memories, but because she had changed completely; she was all skin and bones and her face was ravaged by exhaustion. She insisted we have a drink together. She got straight to the point and told me she was dying. I was sad for her but didn't understand what I could do. Then she showed me a picture of Declan. If she hadn't have been ill, I never would have known I had a son. She raised him all alone, asking nothing of anyone . . . When you called me, I had just received the results of the paternity test and was packing my suitcases to go to Galway so I could be with her until the end.

He stood up and walked toward the sea. I was freezing, not because the temperature had dropped, but because of what I had just heard. Life had given him a son he hadn't wanted and whose mother had died; and life had taken away my daughter, my reason for living. Clara was Declan's age when she'd gone. And yet, I was far from being envious. How was he going to manage? A man who was a loner, scarred by his own mother's death and his father's desertion?

"Diane, we have to get going. Jack and Abby eat early."

I walked ten paces behind him as we headed for his car. My heart ached when I got into his Range Rover. As well as the various rubbish that always Edward left, there were now traces of a child. Another difference: his car smelled less like tobacco than before. It was a short ride; he drove as fast as ever. Once the car was parked and the engine turned off, Edward leaned back in his seat, closed his eyes and sighed.

"Edward . . . I . . . "

"Please, don't say anything."

He got out of the car; so did I. As we went into Abby and Jack's house, we were greeted by a child's laughter, laughter that brought tears to my eyes. I was careful, so no one noticed. Edward just stroked his son's hair. I took over from

Abby in the kitchen; that kept me busy and far away from the child who was always watching me out of the corner of his eye.

Abby presided when we sat down to eat; Jack sat next to me and Edward and his son opposite. The situation was totally bizarre. What was I doing there? I had no choice but to face reality. And to listen to Declan, who talked nonstop. The problem became more serious when he targeted me.

"Where do you live, Diane? Why are you here?"

I looked up and caught Edward looking at me before looking at his son.

"I'm visiting Abby and Jack, and I live in Paris."

"Is that where you went, daddy?"

I clutched the edge of the table when I heard him say that word: "daddy."

"Yes, Declan. That's where I went."

"And did you see daddy, Diane?"

"A little."

"Are you friends, then?"

I looked at Edward, begging him to answer.

"Diane is more Judith's friend. That's enough now, eat up and stop talking."

Declan scowled and looked at his father with a mixture of fear and admiration.

When the meal was over, I hurried to clear the table. Except that Declan, a little boy who had been brought up well, helped me. I didn't want to be unpleasant to him; he'd asked nothing of me and done nothing wrong, but it was more than I could take. Children are like dogs: the less you want to see them, the more they follow you around. Fortunately, Jack came in.

"You've done enough tonight; go out and have your cigarette," he said, winking at me.

"Thanks."

I was already at the entrance by the front door when I overheard Abby and Edward talking. He had an offer of work the day after tomorrow and no one could pick Declan up from school. Abby couldn't do it; she had medical tests scheduled 50 kilometers from Mulranny. With a gentleness I'd never seen in him, Edward reassured her, saying that it wasn't important. I walked away thinking the complete opposite.

While I was smoking my cigarette, I took advantage of the time to call Olivier. To my great surprise, he was spending the evening with Felix. After being reassured about the state of the bookshop, I couldn't help telling him what I'd learned that day, and it worried him.

"How does he seem?"

"It isn't easy. I wasn't expecting this."

In the background, I could hear Felix pressing Olivier with questions; Olivier finally explained everything to him. Felix let out an outraged cry and grabbed the telephone.

"Are you joking? He has a kid? When I think that he was about to live with . . . "

"Felix!" I shouted into the phone to stop him talking.

"Oops! Anyway, he was a real bastard to the mother!"

"He didn't know, Felix," I said, defending Edward, which troubled me. "Put Olivier back on now."

He did as he was told, grumbling, but I didn't care.

"Are you happy to be there, in spite of everything?"

"Yes, I am. I'm enjoying Abby and Jack, and Judith will be arriving soon; don't worry about me."

"I miss you, Diane."

"Me too."

The front door opened behind me. Edward and his son were going home.

"I have to go," I said to Olivier. "Lots of love."

"Me too."

I hung up. Edward was staring at me, clenching his teeth. Declan came straight at me.

"Will we see each other again?"

"I don't know . . . "

"It would be fun; we could play with Postman Pat."

"Declan, leave Diane in peace and get in the car!"

"But . . . "

"No buts."

Father and son were wary of each other. In spite of his harshness, Edward seemed helpless.

"You're mean, daddy!"

He ran to the car. Edward sighed.

"I'm sorry if he bothered you tonight."

"Not at all. Don't worry."

The spontaneity of my reply surprised me. Did I say it because I didn't want Edward to worry or was I defending the child?

"Good night," he said.

"You too."

He smiled ironically—I didn't understand why—and went

to join his son, who was sulking, his face glued to the car window.

A little later, when I was going to bed, I no longer knew how I felt. I was touched by their pain. In spite of all the defenses I'd constructed around me, I couldn't be insensitive to their situation. That little boy had lost his mother so recently and was living with a father he didn't know. On the other hand, it was laughable to think of Edward as a father; but it was wrong to laugh about it. Edward must be putting enormous pressure on himself to try to do things properly, but he had no role model and was probably eaten up with guilt. I fell asleep thinking that there was nothing I could do, but it would be difficult for me not to be aware of the drastic change.

6

The next day, Abby decided that I needed to get some fresh air. After lunch, she ordered Jack and me to take advantage of her nap to go for a walk. She had no problem pretending to be tired; I found her more worn out than when she'd gotten up.

"I could go for a walk by myself," I suggested to Jack.

"She'd kick me out as soon as you weren't looking! And I'd really like to stretch my legs with you."

I had to admit that I was as happy as he was that we could to spend some time together. He made sure Abby had everything she needed for the afternoon and that it was within reach; then he kissed her forehead before gesturing for me to follow him. To my great surprise, we took the car. Jack drove to the cottages and parked at the back. He wanted to show me a little part of the Wild Atlantic Way—a road that went along the entire western coast of Ireland. And to think that for nearly a year, it hadn't occurred to me to go further than I could see!

"Take this!"

He took a warm jacket with a hood out of the trunk.

"We're going to get drenched!" he said, smiling.

"Two days with no rain: it was too good to be true!"

We set off on our walk. I didn't even consider talking: the beauty of the landscape and the brilliant colors took my breath away. A year earlier, I had only seen some green, while the entire range of colors in the rainbow were forever there: the dark reds of the peat bog dotted with little purple flowers, the terrifying blackness of the distant mountains, the white sheep, the deep, cold blue of the sea, the sun glistening on the waves. I felt each gust of wind as a gift. Even the rain made me happy when it started to fall. I pulled the hood tighter over my head and continued walking without even thinking of taking shelter. I was no longer the softy of the past. Jack held his hands behind his back and walked at my pace—I didn't have his long legs. He didn't try to make conversation. I could simply sense him, happy to be there with me. Every now and then, passing drivers honked at us; he waved and smiled at the drivers.

"You must have had quite a shock yesterday," he finally said, after we'd been walking for forty-five minutes.

"That's an understatement . . ."

"It had been a very long time since I told Edward off the way I did when he refused to warn you before you got here at the beginning of the week."

"Why did you do that?"

"I didn't want you to feel betrayed. I was afraid you'd leave and that Abby would suffer because of it."

In truth, we'd come close.

"In spite of the telling off, he insisted on being stupid. Stubborn as a mule!"

"That's nothing new! But everything's fine, really."

"Whatever he does, you always end up forgiving him," he said, laughing.

I laughed less. He said no more and we headed back.

As I got my bottom comfortably into the car, I tried to remember if I had ever walked so much in all my life; quite frankly, a hike at two o'clock was not part of my routine. And yet, my legs had held up; I felt light, in tip-top shape. I looked into the mirror on the visor; my cheeks were red, my eyes shining, my hair incredibly damp, but I was breathing in healthy air. People who live by the seaside, even in the Irish weather, have glowing skin. Just look at Jack. If I kept this up, I'd go back even more suntanned than I was after my weekend in the south of France with Olivier. I wanted to finish with a flourish.

"What would you say to a stop at the pub to perk us up?"

"Nothing would please me more!"

Fifteen minutes later, we arrived at the parking lot of the pub. Jack got out of the car without realizing I hadn't moved. I stared at the front of the pub; another place that brought memories to the surface, another place where the good times overshadowed the bad. Jack knocked on my window; I opened the door and got out of the passenger seat.

"Don't you feel the call of the beer?"

"Yes, but it's strange to be here."

"They're not going to believe their eyes! No one has forgotten you!"

"And you think that's a good thing?"

It was here I'd made a scene over Edward, dancing on the bar, so drunk I could barely stand up and was seconds away from getting into a fight with a real bitch . . . In short, I hadn't always shown my most sterling side.

"When will you accept that you're at home here, my little French friend?"

He pushed open the door. Immediately, I could smell beer and wood; the sound of muted conversations reminded me of the tranquility you could find in this place. I walked in, hidden by Jack's wide body.

"Look who I've brought!" he said to the barman, who looked older but still the same.

"I must be dreaming!"

He came out from behind the bar, took me by the shoulders and kissed me on each cheek. I felt so tiny between these two elderly giants!

"So your nephew finally decided to go and bring her back!" he cried, returning to his post.

"Diane came to see Abby."

"Of course, how stupid of me!"

Jack looked at me sadly.

"I'm fine . . . " I said, to reassure him. "And besides, he's not completely wrong: if I hadn't run into Edward in Paris, I certainly wouldn't be here!"

He burst out laughing. So did I. All of Mulranny had

witnessed the many ups and downs of my relationship with Edward, and everyone had their own opinion on the matter!

A pint of Guinness appeared in front of me. I admired its color, the thick, milky foam, the way it smelled like coffee, the ritual of pouring half of it out, then the other half . . . It had been more than a year since I'd had it. The last time was in this very place. Life moved on. Before, Guinness reminded me of Colin, because it was the only beer he liked. That was why I'd come to Mulranny. Today, I no longer thought of my husband when I saw the golden harp that was the symbol of Guinness: I thought of Ireland, of Jack, who drank it at four o'clock instead of tea, of Edward who, without realizing it, had forced me to try it. Drinking it now was a shock; I realized I'd been depriving myself of a great pleasure, out of ignorance. We clinked glasses, Jack winked and looked at me as I took my first sip.

"It's sooo good!"

"Victory," he said to the barman. "She's one of us!"

We spent the next hour talking to various people who recognized me. They came over and asked how I was and what I was doing in a friendly way; we talked about the rain, of course, but also about the summer, which had been a good one, about rugby matches and Gaelic soccer played the weekend before. Then it was time to get back to Abby. That evening, I fizzled out soon after dinner. That day had felt like a week.

Abby and Jack left early the next day for some doctors' appointments. I didn't feel like being alone in their big house, so I decided to take advantage of the day and go for a ramble to Achill Island to continue my exploration of the place from the day before. I took the same route as Jack, passing in front of the cottages, but stopped myself from glancing at them. I drove along the coast, fascinated by the wild countryside and the elements of nature. And yet, I couldn't manage to be totally absorbed and satisfied. I tried to control my mind and my thoughts . . . a bitter failure. I ended up hitting the breaks right in the middle of the road.

"Fucking idiot!" I screamed inside my car.

I got out and slammed the door with all my might. I lit a cigarette and walked through a meadow down to the sea. It was beautiful out, it felt good, I stood over the waves, I had the whole day in front of me to be out in the fresh air, like the day before, but I could only think of one thing. I was shocked . . .

I ran to my car, made a U-turn and headed back to Mulranny as fast as I could, cursing myself the whole time for my stupidity. I stopped right in front of the cottage and knocked on his door. Edward couldn't hide his anxiety when he saw me there.

"What's wrong? Is it Abby?"

"Your job, today. Is it important?"

"What are you talking about?"

"I heard you talking to Abby the other night. Answer me, and quickly, before I change my mind."

"Yes, it is."

"What time does Declan finish school?"

"Three-thirty."

"I'll go get him; go to work. Will you give me your keys?"

"Come in for two minutes."

"No."

He took his bunch of keys from his pocket and handed them to me.

"See you later."

"Wait," he said, taking hold of my arm.

We stared at each other for a long time.

"Thank you."

"No problem."

I whistled for Postman Pat and headed to the beach with him. Five minutes later, I heard Edward's jeep speeding off. I threw a stick for the dog and didn't look back.

Three-thirty came too fast. I'd skipped lunch for fear of throwing up. I'd only opened the door to Edward's cottage to get the dog in, putting off going back into that house. I smoked a cigarette as I walked to the school, calling myself all sorts of names. How could I have come up with such an idea? The last I'd heard, I couldn't bear to see children; they frightened me, petrified me, reminded me of Clara. Edward had asked nothing of me and I owed him nothing. Why had I wanted to help him, do him a favor? Of course he was still important to me, he always would be, that was an indisputable fact, but to go from there to endangering my peace of mind! Was I suddenly becoming voyeuristic over this little boy, his relationship with his father, his sadness, his mourning—perhaps not so different from my own? He'd lost his mother; I'd lost my daughter. I threw my cigarette butt away a few yards from the school. It was horrific; radiant mothers with baby carriages waiting for their older children.

Some of them recognized me from when I'd lived there, and I aroused the same curiosity as before; they looked at me, whispering to each other. I felt like saying: "I'm back, ladies!" Then the bell rang and they disappeared. A flood of children rushed out of the classrooms. It might have been Clara running out, laughing, except that Clara didn't wear a uniform like these little Irish children, who ran all over the place looking for their mothers. Memories ate up my insides; I could hear her calling me: "Mommy, mommy, there you are!" I pictured her looking all sloppy, her hair a mess, bits of paint on her hands and face; I could smell her child's sweaty smell, hear her chirping . . .

"Diane, Diane, there you are!"

I was brutally brought back to reality when Declan saw me.

"My teacher told me you'd been coming to get me, this is so great!"

"Do you want me to carry your schoolbag?"

"Daddy never carries it."

Why wasn't I surprised?

"Well, I will."

He got it off his shoulder and handed it to me. We were leaving the playground when he grabbed my hand and said goodbye to his friends.

He looked so proud. On the way to the cottage, he didn't say anything, undoubtedly waiting for me to start the conversation. I took responsibility; it wasn't his fault; I'd gotten in this situation all by myself. I had to take responsibility, regardless of the consequences.

"So, how was school?"

His face lit up with joy and he enthusiastically launched into what had happened that day. He kept talking as we went inside the house. He threw down his coat—just as messy as his father—and ran into the living room. He started playing with his dog, chattering the whole time. He didn't notice that I'd stopped before entering the room. I was returning to this cottage, to my intimacy with Edward. In less than a few seconds, I took in two important changes: gone were the disgusting ashtrays full of cigarette butts and gone was the photo of Megan on the beach. And yet, it was impossible to imagine that a child lived here: there were no toys, no sign of felt-tip pens. I didn't need proof, it was totally obvious: Edward had no idea what his son needed. I felt bad for both of them. I took off my jacket and hung it on the coat rack in the hall. I went behind the kitchen counter, the place I'd seen Edward stand so many times.

"Declan, would you like a snack?"

"Oh, yes!"

Without much hope, I look around in the cupboards to find the ideal snack, thinking I might have spoken too soon. I was being mean. I was able to make him some hot chocolate and give him some cookies. I watched him as he wolfed them down, fighting against seeing that other image. Declan was sitting on a high stool in his father's kitchen; Clara would have been on the barstool in the bookstore. I tried to reassure myself that their resemblance ended there. Declan no longer had his mother while Clara still had hers. Hers, a mother who was giving a snack to another child, a child who meant nothing to her.

"Do you want to go down to the beach?"

"With Postman Pat?"

"Of course. Do you have any homework?"

He frowned.

"You do your homework and then we'll go, OK?"

He nodded. I went and got his schoolbag before sitting down next to him at the counter. He was in the class that was the equivalent of our kindergarten; I should be able to manage. Clara didn't live long enough to do any homework. I leafed through his notebook: he had to read and understand one page of a book. I would have to be careful of my accent. I put the book between us and he started reading. His attention and concentration astounded me; Clara wouldn't have been so well behaved. When we were done, I asked him to go and change his clothes, of course, before going out. He jumped down from his stool and stared at me.

"Do you need any help?"

"No."

"Is there a problem?"

He shook his head and disappeared upstairs.

On the beach, I just was happy to watch him run around with the dog. I never stopped interrogating myself. How was it that I could take care of this child without breaking down? Was I trying to forgive myself for having left Edward over a year ago through his son? Maybe I could do it because I was leaving in a few days and there would be no consequences in my life? That way I could remain detached from him.

Having no idea when Edward would be getting home, I asked Declan if he wanted to have a shower when we got into the house. He went upstairs without a fight, without asking anything. I waited for about fifteen minutes before going upstairs. This hallway, this bathroom . . . I knocked on the door.

"Everything OK?"

"I do it by myself with daddy."

He was a little man who had no choice but to manage by himself, without expecting anything from anyone.

"Am I allowed to go into your room?"

"Yes."

I smiled sadly when I looked around. Edward had made an effort: there were toys—a racetrack, a train, some Lego, some soft toys thrown here and there on the unmade bed. But the walls were cold, with no decoration. His clothes were half put away in a dresser whose drawers were partly open, the rest still in suitcases. But seeing an armchair in the corner of the room stopped me in my tracks. Declan came in, his pajama top on backwards and his hair still wet.

"Don't move," I said.

I went to get his towel. He was waiting for me in the middle of the room, grinning from ear to ear and looking slightly shy. I rubbed his hair dry and put his top on the right way round. His beautiful eyes tried to send me a message that I refused to try to understand.

"You're perfect now."

He put his arms around my waist, pressed his face against me and hugged me tight. I could barely breathe; I looked into space and kept my arms down at my sides. Suddenly, he let go of me and went to play with his toy cars, laughing and making up stories, rejuvenated by a new feeling of joy.

"I'm going to leave you for five minutes; I'm going outside to have a cigarette."

"Like daddy," he replied, without taking any more notice of me.

I ran down the stairs, grabbed my ciggies, and went outside. I lit my cigarette and called Olivier.

"I'm happy to hear your voice," I said as soon as he'd answered.

"Me too, are you OK? You sound very tired."

Pointless to worry him by explaining what I was doing.

"Tell me how you are, what's happening at the bookstore, in Paris, with Felix."

He spoke enthusiastically. Little by little, he led me back to my home, to my life. He kept my demons at bay by giving me some air. I missed the bookstore and the emotional stability it had given me. Olivier's gentleness, his calming simplicity . . . My breathing space didn't last long; Declan had gone into the living room and was looking for me, visibly upset.

"I'll call you tomorrow."

"I can't wait for you to come back, Diane."

"Me too. Lots of love."

I went back inside. Declan smiled at me, relieved.

"Can I watch TV, please?"

"If you like."

"When will daddy get home?"

"I don't know. Do you want to call him?"

"No!"

"If you want to, you shouldn't be afraid. Daddy will understand . . . "

"No, I want to watch TV."

He was an expert at finding his cartoons. Given the time, I decided to make him supper. I cooked to the sound of his laughter, with Postman Pat at my feet who was waiting for me to drop something he could eat. When I caught myself smiling, I told myself once more that I wasn't really the one doing this.

Three-quarters of an hour later, we'd finished eating—I'd joined Declan—the dishes were done, it was nearly nine o'clock, and there was still no sign of Edward. Declan was on the couch, watching cartoons.

"You're going to have to go to bed," I told him.

He looked upset.

"Ah . . . "

He dragged himself away from the cushions and obediently turned off the television. All the happiness seemed to have drained from his face; he seemed to have withdrawn into himself.

"I'll come up to your room with you."

He nodded. When we got upstairs, he went and brushed his teeth without me having to ask him. I put on the bedside lamp and smoothed out his comforter. When he came in, he got down on all fours and looked for something under his bed. He came out with a big scarf. It wasn't hard to guess whom it had belonged to. Then he got into bed.

"Shall I leave the light on?"

"Yes," he replied, very quietly.

"Sleep tight."

I hadn't taken two steps when I heard him sobbing.

"Stay with me."

Exactly what terrified me. I started by kneeling next to his bed, near his head; he looked out from under the covers and his face was distorted with sadness; he clutched his mother's scarf to him, his wide eyes were full of tears, as if distraught by pain and how much he missed her. I reached toward him, gently, watching him to judge if I was doing the right thing; I stroked his hair. As soon as I touched him, he closed his eyes, then opened them again, begging me to do something to ease his suffering. I asked myself one question. Just one. A forbidden question: what would I have done if he were Clara? In my mind, I begged my daughter to forgive this betrayal; it was with her that I should have been doing this. Do what I had refused to do with her little dead body, tell her that everything was going to be all right, that she'd be fine, that I'd always be there for her. I stretched out alongside Declan and held him tight, breathing in how he smelled, so like a child. He snuggled against me, clung onto me and cried. For a long time, without stopping. He wanted his mother, was calling for her.

"There, there . . . " I whispered.

And then I heard a sound coming from my mouth, a sound I hadn't heard in a very long time: a little lullaby I used to sing to Clara when she had a nightmare. My voice did not quiver, even though tears fell freely down my face. We were both crying for the same loss. We were in the same place, an abyss where we suffered because we missed someone so much. Little by little, Declan's sobbing subsided.

"Are you a mother, Diane?" he asked me, hiccoughing.

"What makes you say that?"

"Because you do the same things my mother did . . . "

Children have a sixth sense when it comes to finding a weakness. This little boy proved that my actions, my words were imbued, branded by motherhood, by the person I used to be, whether I liked it or not.

"I used to be a mother . . . "

"Why used to?"

"My little girl, Clara . . . she went away like your mother."

"Do you think they're together?"

"Maybe."

"My mommy will be kind to her, so don't worry."

I hugged him close and rocked him, crying silently.

"Can you sing the song again?"

I sang. He breathed more easily.

An hour went by before I heard the front door open. Edward called out to me; I didn't reply for fear of waking Declan, who was still in my arms; I hadn't let go of him for a second. Edward climbed the stairs four at a time and froze when he got to the doorway of his son's room. He leaned onto the doorframe for support, clenched his fists, looked towards the heavens, clearly wishing to flee the scene. He, too, was suffering in this situation. I understood why the armchair was in the room; he must have slept there, to watch over Declan. I gave him a look that ordered him to be quiet. In his sleep, Declan struggled slightly when I let go of him. I placed his mother's scarf as close to his face as I could, and stopped myself from kissing his forehead. I'd done enough. I walked out past Edward, who looked exhausted. He followed me downstairs. I put on my jacket and opened the front door. I was walking away when he decided to speak.

"I'm really sorry I got back so late. I should have spared you that."

"I have to go."

"Thank you for taking care of Declan."

I gestured it was nothing, still with my back to him.

"Diane, look at me."

"No."

He gently took my arm, turned me around, and saw that my face was covered in tears.

"What happened? What's wrong?"

He was about to take my face in his strong hands when I quickly pulled away.

"Don't touch me . . . please. Nothing's wrong, nothing happened. Declan was adorable."

I ran to my car and drove as fast as I could to Jack and Abby's. I spent a long time in floods of tears over the steering wheel. Children brought too much suffering, too much pain, whether they were living or dead. Declan's pain was unbearable to me; I so wanted to be able to help him, but it was more than I could manage, and I refused to betray Clara. She would think I was abandoning her again. I'd abandoned her when I let her go in the car, I'd abandoned her when I hadn't said goodbye, I couldn't abandon her by playing at being a mother to Declan, or any other child. I had no right.

When I went into the living room, I found Abby, in her bathrobe, sitting in a rocking chair in front of the fire. She gestured for me to come closer. I staggered over to her, collapsed to the ground and put my head on her knees. She stroked my hair as I stared at the flames.

"I want my daughter, Abby."

"I know . . . you're so brave. I'm sure you did Declan a lot of good."

"He's in so much pain."

"Like you."

Several minutes passed.

"What about you? How did it go at the doctor's?"

"I'm tired. I'm slowly fading away."

I hugged her knees more tightly.

"No, not you . . . You don't have the right to leave us."

"It's natural that I go, Diane. And I'll watch over all of them. Put your mind at rest. Have a cry now; you'll feel better."

I decided to spend the next day with Abby and Jack. I felt the need to focus on the main reason for my trip to Mulranny and not think about Declan and his father. The days were speeding by; my time with Abby was coming to an end. Judith was arriving in less than twenty-four hours, then it would be over. Abby was tired by the day before, so we spent the whole day at home. In the late afternoon, Jack went for a walk on the beach. He couldn't spend an entire day locked in the house; the call of the fresh air was stronger than anything.

We were both settled in the living room with a cup of tea.

"What are your plans?" she asked me.

"Oh . . . I don't really know . . . I think I'll just keep going the way I have. I like it in my bookstore; I own it now . . . "

"And what about your fiancé?

She smiled at me.

"Olivier isn't my fiancé, Abby."

"Ah, young people today! Are you happy with him? Is he good to you, at least?"

"I couldn't have found anyone kinder or more considerate."

"That's a good thing . . . I hope that Edward will find the same happiness as you . . ."

She stared straight at me. I knew what she was thinking, and I refused to have that conversation.

"Please, Abby . . ."

"Don't worry, I won't make myself a nuisance. But we worry so much about him and Declan. Edward suffered a great deal when he lost his mother, and also by the horrible way my brother, his father, behaved . . . When I see him today . . . I know what he'll do to make sure he doesn't make the same mistakes: he'll put his son before himself."

"He's strong; I'm sure he'll cope . . ."

Her attachment to Edward and Judith was as deep as if she were their real mother. There was a question I was dying to ask her.

"Is it because you were taking care of them that you and Jack never had any children?"

"No . . . it was so long ago, and yet . . ."

She gazed out into the distance, overwhelmed by a wave of sadness.

"We lost two babies. I never had the chance to spend any time with them, but I understand your suffering over your little girl . . ."

Tears came to my eyes.

"Abby, I'm so sorry; I shouldn't have . . . "

"It's fine . . . we have something in common and I know it's the right time to talk to you about it. Before, when you lived here, would have been too soon, but today . . . maybe it will help you . . . "

"How did you manage to take care of children who weren't your own?"

"Oh, there was a lot of shouting and tears! At the beginning, I didn't want to allow myself to be Judith's mother; I just wanted to be her aunt, and most especially, I didn't want to think I was stealing someone else's children. I was distant to her. She made things easy for me by being a good baby, too good. She didn't cry, never demanded anything; she could stay in her bed and not make a sound. When you think how she turned out . . . "

She stopped talking and laughed. So did I. Imagining Judith quiet and subdued seemed absurd.

"Now Edward was another story . . . He goaded us . . . threw one fit after the other, broke everything . . . "

Nothing unusual there.

"Jack knew how to manage him, but I did nothing; I didn't want to see that he was crying out for me to help him and his sister."

"What happened to change things?"

"My wonderful Jack . . . One evening, after Edward flew into a rage for the hundredth time, he threatened to send them back to my brother, because I really didn't want to take care of them. For the only time in our life, we slept in separate rooms that night. I realized I was about to lose everything: my husband and my children—because, yes, they *were* my children. The good Lord had sent them to me and no one considered me a thief . . . "

"You're an amazing woman . . . "

"No more amazing than any woman . . . you'll get there too, you will."

"I don't think so . . . "

"Let life do its work."

Abby and Jack spent the entire evening sharing their memories with me by showing me their photo albums. I was coming to understand this family's history.

7

I heard Judith before I saw her.

"Where is she, the little slut?" she shouted from the front door.

"We warned you she was in good form!" Jack said as he entered the living room.

I stood up from the couch to watch her arrival. She spotted me, pointed her finger at me, saying: "You, you, you," over and over again. Then, without sparing me her piercing look, she planted a big kiss on Jack's cheek before heading for me.

"You little . . . you're nothing more than a . . . oh, shit!"

She threw her arms around me and gave me a big hug.

"You know you're going to get an earful from me, don't you?"

"And I missed you too, Judith."

She let go of me, sniffled, took me by the shoulders, and looked me up and down.

"You've got some flesh on your bones. Wow!"

"And you're just as spectacular as ever!"

"I'm keeping the legend alive."

It was the absolute truth. Judith looked amazing, unbelievably sexy, with a mischievous look in her eyes that would melt the toughest of men. Even her brother was prey in her trap. Abby came over and hugged us both. Judith gave me a wink that was both affectionate and complicit.

"I have my two daughters with me."

My uneasiness must have been apparent.

"Don't make that face, Diane. What Abby said is true. And besides, you were this close to becoming my sister . . . "

I'd forgotten how formidable they were when they ganged up together. We all burst out laughing.

That day was spent as if we were at a reunion. We took turns laughing, crying, and hearing Judith tease me. Judith and I shared the task of consoling Abby. She looked ten years younger; in just a few hours, every trace of her illness had disappeared: her face was relaxed, she had all her energy back and she no longer seemed depressed. Judith and I had to fight with her so she'd let us take care of making supper, that's how well she felt. That evening, two more people would be joining us: Edward and Declan. I refused to think about it.

A large part of the afternoon was taken up with preparing the meal; I got a real lesson in Irish gastronomy, learning how to make rye bread and authentic Irish stew. At that moment,

I thought they were right: I was with my mother and sister. A sister with whom I'd been doing silly things as if we were fifteen years old, and our mother who told us off. Every now and again, Jack tried to enter our ladies' den, but invariably turned back.

Judith got out her cell phone to immortalize the moment. Abby took part in the fun, laughing, and so did I. We took selfies of the three of us in gales of laughter. I was playing the fool when the door opened. Declan and Edward.

"Judith!" cried Declan.

"Hey, if it isn't my favorite little snotty-nosed kid! Now, what did I tell you?"

"Hello, Aunt Judith," he obediently replied, before throwing his arms around her neck.

Hearing this made me laugh so hysterically that doubled over. I hadn't laughed so hard in years.

"Has anyone ever seen Diane in such a state?" asked Abby, also in stitches.

"It's Judith's fault!" I managed to say. "Aren't you ashamed of yourself? You put your feet on the table and then make him call you that?"

"Wait, I'll try to be more classy."

Edward followed my lead, laughing as well. It was the first time since I'd seen him again that he looked relaxed and smiling. I wanted to look away. I did, but met Declan's gaze. He was still clinging onto Judith. He gave me a big smile and waved.

"Hello, Declan." I said softly.

"Now, boys and girls, back to work! Girls, in the kitchen; Edward, you're going to take some real pictures of us!" Abby ordered.

He looked at her as if she were from outer space.

"Use your talent for your family, for once. Do it for me."

"Only because it's for you," he grumbled.

He was about to leave the kitchen when Declan called him.

"Daddy, wait!"

Everyone looked at him. He squirmed out of Judith's arms so his feet hit the ground. She finally let him go.

"Can I help you?" he asked Edward, going over to him.

"Come to the car with me."

The way he smiled at his father made it clear how much he already loved him. A few minutes later, he was Edward's assistant, handing him whatever he needed. Judith's clowning around and the simple pleasure of making Abby happy were enough to block out my uneasiness at their presence, or at least to come to terms with it. Jack also joined us, pouring us each some Guinness. He sat down and clinked glasses with his wife. Declan ran around the table laughing. Judith cleared away all the mess and I took charge of washing the dishes. We were all talking at the same time, about everything and nothing, simply excited by the joy of being there. When I'd finished the dishes, I leaned against the kitchen counter and drank my beer. I caught Edward looking at me—I felt that time had stopped. I wanted to look away, but couldn't. What could he be thinking about? As for me, it was impossible to clearly know what was running through my mind. Then, suddenly, he clenched his teeth and the bubble burst. He was looking for his son; Declan was staring at his father's camera on the kitchen counter as if it were some kind of treasure.

"Don't touch; it's easily broken."

You could see the disappointment on the little boy's face. It was even worse when Edward went outside to put everything away in the car without asking him to help and without saying a word to anyone. He was gone for ages, which seemed to make Declan anxious. He stared at the kitchen door, jumped at the slightest sound, as if he were keeping watch. When he heard his father come back inside the house, his face relaxed and he could smile again.

When we went to sit down at the table, Declan insisted on sitting next to me. There was no way I could refuse. After all I'd already gone through, I could manage that. Edward was about to scold him but I stopped him.

"It's fine," I said, smiling.

The atmosphere during dinner was fun, convivial, and domestic. Life had spared no one at the table, the others most especially, given Abby's recent illness. Yet everyone tried to bounce back, to live, to be content to have some happy moments; a mixture of the instinct to survive and an acceptance of fatality. They'd welcomed me with all my screw-ups and still did. I was with them and it felt good. But a part of me would have preferred to feel less at home; the separation was going to be difficult, I already knew that. The more I needed to move forward with my life in Paris—to be sure I had completely erased the past—the more complicated it would be to think of them so far away. That was the ironic effect of this reunion. Judith forced me out of my shell.

"Should we head to the pub later?"

"If you like."

"Out of the question to miss an opportunity to live it up with you! On the other hand, try not to end up the way you did last time!"

"If you could manage not to remind me of that scene, I'd be grateful."

But given the malicious smile on her face, I understood she wasn't going to stop there. She elbowed Edward.

"Hey, bro, you remember when we had to go and get her?"

He murmured something quietly. Both he and I remembered it perfectly.

"Tell us what happened, children," Abby cut in, all excited.

"Diane could barely stand up. Edward gave it to some guy who was all over her. He had to carry her out over his shoulder. You would have died laughing; she was waving her arms and legs all over the place trying to fight him but Edward didn't budge; he was unstoppable."

Abby and Jack looked at us, one after the other, then burst out laughing. We also looked at each other, embarrassed at first, but finally joining in with the general laughter.

"What does that mean, to give him one?" Declan asked.

"It means to fight," Judith replied.

"Wow, daddy, you got into a fight?"

"As if it had been the only time . . . " Jack chipped in. "Your father was already getting into fights when he was your age, sonny!"

"Why are you telling him that?" Edward replied.

"Will you teach me, daddy?"

Father and son looked at each other. For the first time, Edward gave an affectionate look to Declan before turning to his sister.

"Go now, if you like, I'll clean up here."

He stood up, stroked his son's hair and asked him to help clear the table. It was more than I could bear; I stared at them until they disappeared into the kitchen. Judith cleared her throat.

"Ready to rave it up?"

"More than ready!"

We each kissed Abby and Jack, who thanked us for such a wonderful evening. Edward and Declan came out of the kitchen and Judith went over to kiss them. All I did was give them a wave.

"Be sensible," Edward told us.

"You won't have to get into a fight tonight," I replied in a flash.

And immediately regretted what I'd said.

We got to the pub laughing and fooling around. Once inside, I couldn't help thinking out loud.

"It feels so good to be here!"

"I knew you'd come back," Judith said, teasing me.

The barman gave us a big wave from behind the counter. We walked over to him, even though there was nowhere to sit. In a flash, he got us seated: he used his authority to move two customers so we could have their barstools. Without even asking us, he brought us each a pint of Guinness. Saturday night in the pub with live music. The band kept playing and everyone enjoyed it. We joined the other customers who were

singing as loud as they could. I was back in the atmosphere I
had loved so much . . . and which I hadn't appreciated enough
the year before.

"I've got an extremely important question to ask you," Judith suddenly said.

"I'm listening."

"Is Felix still gay?"

I burst out laughing.

"More than ever," I finally managed to say.

"Shit! Because he's the man of my dreams, you do realize
that, don't you?"

She took me by the arm and led me back to our seats at the
bar where she ordered our third or fourth pint, I was beginning to lose track! In the fifteen minutes that followed, I was
treated to the latest adventures of Judith-who-falls-in-love-
every-other-day. My phone rang, interrupting our conversation. It was Olivier.

"Two seconds," I said, then turning to Judith, "Sorry . . . "

She gave me a mocking smile and nodded toward the place
outside where all the smokers were gathered. I grabbed my
cigarettes and walked through the pub, followed closely by
Judith, who started talking to the other smokers.

"Ok! I'm here."

"Where are you? It's so noisy!"

"At the pub with Judith. There's live music every Saturday
night."

"You found your friend?"

"Yes, and we had a fantastic day. Abby was so happy, it
was wonderful!"

"You feel good there . . . "

I felt a pang of guilt run through me; I'd forgotten to call him today because I was so happy to be with Judith again.

"I do . . . but what about you, how are you?"

"Everything's fine here, all OK. I'm at home now, hanging around all by myself. I won't bother you any more . . . "

"You're not bothering me, idiot!"

"Have a great time. I just wanted to know that you were all right. And now I know! Lots of love."

· "To you too. Until tomorrow; I'll call you tomorrow, promise."

Judith must have been keeping an eye on me because as soon as I'd put my phone back in my pocket, she was right next to me.

"So, how's your man?"

"He's fine. Should we go back inside?"

We went back to our seats at the bar; it was as if we were the guests of honor. Judith wasn't going to drop the subject.

"Is it serious between you?"

"I don't know, I think so . . . yes . . . in fact, it is . . . "

"But what about my brother?"

"What do you mean?"

"You don't love him any more? And don't try to tell me you didn't love him before because I won't believe you."

"Oh, Judith, please . . . "

"We really do need to have this conversation!"

I sighed.

"I wasn't ready for a relationship with him; I would have hurt him even more some day if I'd stayed."

"And now?"

"Now more than a year has gone by. I started my life in Paris over again, I'm at home there, and I met someone I feel good with."

"I understand. I'm happy for you."

She finished her pint in one long gulp and ordered another round, but not without shooting me a sideways look.

"What do you want to say?"

"Well, it still must be really weird to see him again!"

"I can't deny that . . . But Judith, stop right now, don't make it into a big thing . . . "

"OK, OK! But you won't convince me that you're not dying of curiosity and want to know more . . . "

"You're right . . . I'm worried about him . . . "

"You're not the only one!"

"I know . . . "

"He deserves more than to be stuck with his son! How can he possibly get on with his life now?"

"Is Declan being here a problem for you?"

"Of course not. How could you not love that kid? I'm simply fed up seeing my bro getting tied up with one hassle after another. He's jinxed! This isn't a reproach, Diane, but he really was a fucking mess after you left . . . "

I hung my head in shame. I had a flashback to the moment I told him I was leaving. I'd caused him so much suffering.

"He threw himself into his work, body and soul; he was always off somewhere, he left Mulranny and everything that could remind him of you. It was painful, but the right thing to do in the end; he was really cracking up. And then, bang, he runs into Declan's mother! His first reaction was to see himself as the bad guy in the whole business . . . you know how principled he is! Fortunately, she was a good woman, serious and understanding. She never wanted Edward to know about it, she took away his sense of guilt and also brought him out of his shell, to be sure she could really entrust their son to him."

"I can understand her doing that; she didn't really know him, after all!"

I took a big gulp of beer and sighed.

"But how is he, really? How does he feel about the situation he's in?"

"Diane, are you living in la-la land or something? Do you think he pours out his heart about his state of mind?"

I couldn't control myself and burst out laughing.

"You see, you *are* curious!" she continued, laughing as well.

"You're right! Happy now?"

"Absolutely! Listen though, what I can tell you is that he went slightly off the rails when he got the results of the paternity test. It had been years since I'd seen him in such a state!"

"Meaning?"

"He got well and truly plastered and locked himself in his house. It's a miracle he didn't drop down dead. I had to climb through the window to get inside. And then, I had to listen to him rambling on for hours . . . he ranted about everything: our father, that bitch Megan, Abby being sick, and you, you, you! Even though you'd left six months before and no one was allowed to mention your name without starting a nuclear war. He talked about your phone calls and messages . . . "

I was startled; it all happened around the time I'd called . . .

"And now?" I asked.

"He's more alive because of his son; he's going to dedicate his life to him . . . he loves him madly, but what always makes him feel sick is the fact that he gave a child to a woman he didn't love."

"I'd so like to do something to help him . . . "

"Don't pity him."

"That has nothing to do with it . . . "

She smiled wryly.

"I know that very well; I was teasing you . . . No matter what you say, there will always be something between you two; that's just the way it is. You've both made your choices, you and him. You have someone. And he has his son, and that's enough for him. But I think it would do you both a lot of good to talk about it . . . Come on, now; let's have another round of drinks!"

Another pint. Judith had matured; she was much more responsible and clear-headed than before. Which didn't prevent her from getting me to dance to the devilish rhythms of traditional Irish music.

The pub was getting ready to close. Fortunately, we were just a five-minute walk from Jack and Abby's. Both as tipsy as the other, we walked back, arm in arm. I sobered up in less than two seconds when I saw Edward's car still parked in front of the house.

"Why's he still hanging around here?" Judith shouted while burping, showing off her legendary touch of class.

We tiptoed in and headed for the living room. A small

lamp was lit on a side table. I finally made out that Edward was sitting on the couch, his feet on the coffee table, holding a drink in one hand, the other on his son's back, who was sleeping with his head on his father's lap.

"Why are you still here?" Judith asked.

He didn't bother to turn around and look at us to answer.

"Declan had a fit of anxiety when he realized he wouldn't be seeing you two again. The only way to calm him down was to promise him we'd wait for you. He ended up falling asleep."

"You should have called us," I said, walking over to him.

"Thank you, Diane, but I didn't want to screw up your evening."

Judith knelt down next to them and saw the small amount of whiskey left in the bottle. She winked at her brother who smiled sadly.

"Leave him with us tonight; he can sleep with me. Go and sleep in your own bed for once. We'll bring him back around noon tomorrow."

"Well, this may surprise you, but I won't say no."

Judith stood up; Edward took his son in his arms and also got up. Declan clung onto his neck.

"Daddy?"

"Judith and Diane are here; you're going to sleep in Judith's bed with her tonight."

I watched the three of them go upstairs. Their life was so different from mine. To keep busy, I picked up the glass and bottle and put them in the kitchen. I leaned against the sink and drank a glass of water. I jumped when I heard Edward's voice.

"I'm going now."

I turned around; he threw me his pack of cigarettes from across the room; he already had one lit. I understood the message and followed him. After we were outside and I'd taken one, I gave him back his cigarettes. He stared into my eyes and got out his lighter; I leaned down toward the flame, hoping I wouldn't get burned, in both senses of the word. Then he took a few steps into the garden before coming back to me again. He rummaged around in his pocket and took out his car keys. He handed them to me and I instinctively took them.

"Could you drive my son back with my car tomorrow?"

"You're not really going to walk home? It will take you at least half an hour."

"I drank too much, I can't drive . . . it will do me good to get some fresh air."

Our eyes met for a long time. There was so much sadness in his expression, but a touch of anger as well. Nothing would ever appease him.

"Goodnight, Diane."

"Be careful on your way home."

I watched him until he disappeared into the night. I put out my cigarette stub in the ashtray, went back inside, and locked the door. I went upstairs, feeling emotional, ill at ease. Judith's door opened a little.

"Is he still sleeping?" I asked in a whisper.

"Like a rock. Besides asking you to bring back his car, what did he say?"

"Nothing."

"It's just as I said; you two really should talk . . . "

"Goodnight, Judith."

I slipped under the duvet, knowing that sleep would not come quickly. The image of Edward walking away, alone in the darkness, turned around and around in my mind, as well as the way he'd looked at me. Judith was right. There would always be a link between us, a tie we had to unravel as soon as possible so we could both move on.

You might think that the sole purpose of this trip to Ireland was to teach me what a family really is. When I went downstairs for breakfast, I found Abby, in her bathrobe, busy preparing an "Irish breakfast" for us; you could smell the bacon, eggs, and toast. Jack, Judith, and Declan were at the table; I was the only one missing. And yet, something was wrong; you could feel it.

"Wait, let me help you," I suggested to Abby.

"No, my darling, I'm not an invalid!"

"Don't insist; she's already told me to get lost," Judith said.

"Diane," Declan said to me, sobbing.

I looked at him more closely; the terribly sad expression on his face broke my heart. He stood up and came over to me. I instinctively knelt down to his level.

"What's wrong?"

"When is daddy coming back? Why isn't he here?"

"Judith explained everything to you, didn't she?"

"He doesn't believe us," she clarified.

"Declan, your daddy is at home, asleep, he was tired."

"Really?"

"Promise."

He threw himself against me and hung onto my neck. I held my breath. This child was pushing me beyond my limits. Except that I was an adult. I normally had the ability to control my pain, unlike him. In any case, it seemed I was rediscovering my strength and was able to help him.

"Look at me, Declan."

He pulled very slightly away. I had the impression I was looking at his father. I forced that image out of my mind and concentrated on the child he was. I dried his cheeks with my hands.

"He hasn't gone away. We're going to see him after breakfast, all right?"

He nodded.

"Come and sit down."

He instinctively sat down next to me. The food was on our plates and cups filled. Declan was still huddled up.

"Everything is fine, I told you. Trust me. So eat."

Throughout our little talk, I hadn't paid attention to what was happening. Everyone was staring at us. Abby smiled at me sweetly. I chose not to react and dug into my scrambled eggs.

An hour later, Judith let me drive the Jeep. As I parked in front of Edward's cottage, I spotted him and his dog on the beach; he was smoking a cigarette. Declan was overexcited in the back of the car so Judith opened his door as fast as she could. He jumped out in a flash and ran toward his father, who turned around when he heard him call to him. Declan leapt into his arms, Edward lifted him up and gave him a big hug. Then he put him down, knelt down, ruffled his hair, and started talking to him. Declan was waving his arms about to explain something to him while Postman Pat was yapping and rushing all around them. Edward calmed the dog down and smiled at his son, a real smile, the kind of smile he was capable of when he was happy and relieved.

Watching them really shook me up; they were both so handsome and touching. Edward had truly become a father, there was no longer any doubt. He was awkward, subdued, but passionately attached to his child. At that moment, I felt that nothing was more important to him than having found his little boy. As I well understood . . . He must have been really exhausted to leave him with us the night before. Being apart seemed difficult for both of them. Judith joined them but I stayed back until my tears stopped flowing. Brother and sister hugged each other. I walked slowly toward them. Judith ran off down the beach, quickly followed by Declan and Postman Pat. You might wonder which one was the child, the aunt or her nephew. I walked over to Edward and handed him his car keys. One night would not be enough to get him back in shape.

"I didn't crash it."

"I trust you. Shall we go for a little walk?"

"Yes."

We covered more than 100 meters without saying a word, our hands in our pockets; I could hear Declan's cries of joy and the dog's barking in the distance.

"Come this way, we'll sit here; it's the perfect place to watch Judith fooling around."

We sat down beside each other on a rock that overlooked the beach.

"How can I know when he's all right?"

I looked at him; he was staring at his son.

"When you take him in your arms the way you did this morning, he's fine; he knows he has a father. When he can't go to sleep because he wants his mother, he's in pain."

"I'm really sorry you had to go through that."

"Stop; it doesn't matter."

"What did you say to him? It was the only night he didn't have any nightmares since he's been with me."

"Not much; I just talked to him about Clara. That's all."

My voice quivered a little; I lit a cigarette, trembling slightly. Edward gave me a few minutes to compose myself before continuing.

"Ever since we've known each other, you're the only person who never tried to spare my feelings, so I'm counting on you. Tell me what I'm doing wrong with him? I want him to be happy, to forget; I don't want him to end up like me."

My hand took his and squeezed it tightly, as if it had a mind of its own.

"He'll never forget, you always have to remember that. A mother, like a child, is never forgotten. You're not doing anything wrong with him. You're learning, that's all. I have no advice to give you. All parents make mistakes. Give yourself time to come to terms with it. The only thing I know is that Declan looks up to you as if you were some god, and that the idea of losing you terrifies him. I know you . . . you don't say much, but reassure him as much as you can. Spend time with him . . . teach him photography, it's magical to him when he sees you holding your camera, at least, that's how it looked yesterday . . . And . . . if he ends up like you, he'll be very lucky."

I squeezed his hand one last time and let go. I stood up, climbed down from the rock and walked toward the waves. I looked at Declan and Judith in the distance, conscious of the presence of Edward behind me. I breathed in deeply. The wind whipped my face. One thing was sure: I wouldn't end this trip unscathed.

"When are you leaving?" he asked. I hadn't heard him come and stand behind me.

"The day after tomorrow."

"We'll come and say goodbye after school."

"If you like."

He walked away; I watched him take his son and his dog home. They climbed into the car and sped off in a cloud of dust. Judith came over to me, put her arm around my neck and leaned her head against mine.

"Are you OK?"

"Let's say I am."

The rest of the day sped by. Judith and I knew we had little time together. She used the best defense anyone could against sadness: laughter. While we were having lunch at Abby and Jack's, she made sure the fun continued by telling silly jokes. I walked her to her car when it was time for her to set off for Dublin.

"Shall we avoid having a year go by with no contact with each other?"

"I'd really love to come to see you in Paris, but with Abby, I'd be afraid of breaking my promise. So . . . "

"I'll call you," I replied. "Keep me posted about her health."

"That I can do."

Judith's armor cracked; she raised her eyes to the heavens, failing to hide her tears. I took her in my arms.

"Everything will be all right; you'll manage," I whispered in her ear.

"You're really a dumbass! You manage to make me cry . . . You know, it doesn't matter at all who you spend your life with . . . you're still my . . . "

"I know . . . and I feel exactly the same way . . . "

She pulled free, brushed the tears from her cheeks and gave me the thumbs up.

"Come on, Judith, that's enough, you're not a little girl!" she scolded herself. "When you have to leave, you have to leave!"

"Be careful driving."

She gave me a military salute, got into her car, and drove off.

I spent the entire day with Abby. She asked me if I would do her nails and hair; she still wanted to look attractive and didn't dare ask Judith out of modesty. She'd noticed that I was taking good care of myself again and decided I was the perfect one for the job. Our intimacy as women brought us even closer together. We were in Abby and Jack's bedroom. Photos of Edward and Judith decorated the tops of the dressers. Seeing them in school uniforms made me smile.

"Are you happy you came to see us?" Abby asked while I was polishing her nails, both of us sitting on her bed.

"Of course I am! No need to worry."

"And Edward?"

"They're going to stop in to say goodbye after school, at least, that's what he said yesterday . . . "

"And that's it?"

"Umm, yes . . . "

We were interrupted by Jack calling me from downstairs. Declan and his father had just arrived, in fact. It was time to say our goodbyes. Abby went down with me, holding onto my arm; I could feel her perceptive eyes watching me. Once down the stairs, she let go of me to sit in her armchair, exchanging a glance with Jack that did not bode well.

"Hi," was all I said to Declan and Edward.

I couldn't look at his father so decided to make eye contact with his son, who came up to me to give me a kiss.

"Did you have a good day at school?"

"Yes!"

"Come here, my boy, I have something to show you," Jack shouted.

Declan ran off. I had no choice but to turn toward Edward.

"Have a good trip back to Paris," was all he said.

"Thanks."

"It's a shame the two of you didn't see more of each other," Abby said subtly.

"That's very true!" Jack added. "Wouldn't you young things like to go to the pub tonight? We can take care of Declan."

We stared at each other.

"Would you like that?" Edward asked.

"Uh . . . yes, I would."

"Daddy?"

We hadn't noticed that Declan had come over to us again.

"Are you leaving, daddy?"

Edward's shoulders drooped; he stroked his son's hair and smiled at him.

"No . . . don't worry, we'll go home . . . Diane, I'm really sorry . . . We'll do it another time . . . "

We both knew that wasn't true.

"It's normal; I understand."

"Well, maybe . . . Would you like to come and have dinner with us at home?"

"Oh . . . "

I automatically turned to Abby and Jack, as if I needed their permission. They looked at me with all their usual sweet kindness.

"Don't you worry about us."

"You'll come and eat at the house?" Declan insisted, "Say yes!"

I noticed the affectionate way Edward looked at his son. And that made me give in.

"OK, I'll come."

"See you soon," said Edward. "Ready to go, Declan?"

They kissed Abby and Jack and set off. I stood very still in the middle of the living room for several minutes.

"Come here, my darling," Abby called, which fortunately pulled me out of my trance.

I flopped down on the couch; she got up and came over to sit next to me, taking my hand in hers.

"What are you two trying to make me do? You're real schemers!"

Jack burst out laughing.

"She's the main culprit," he said, pointing to his wife.

"You're just as bad!" she immediately replied, smiling.

"What good will it do?"

"It will settle things," said Abby.

"Perhaps, but this is our last night together."

She patted my hand.

"Diane. Even if you'd spent the evening with us, you would have just thought about them all night, and you know that's true, deep down. And we've had a lot of time with you . . . Don't worry . . . And besides, when you're with them, it's almost as if you're with us, and you're good for them, as well . . . "

I leaned my head on her shoulder and enjoyed her maternal warmth.

"I'm going to miss you . . . so very, very much . . . " I whispered.

Jack, who was standing behind the couch, put his hand on my head in a very fatherly way.

"We'll miss you too, my little French darling, but you'll come back . . . "

"Yes . . . "

I leaned in more closely to Abby.

An hour later, I left them, promising to have a good evening without worrying about them. When I was almost at the cottage, I decided to take one last walk along the beach before joining Edward and his son. I wanted to feel the sea, this landscape, this wind rush through me one more time. Getting some fresh air would do me the world of good. I didn't know what to think of the evening that lay ahead. There was something troubling about having dinner with Declan and Edward; I was intruding in their closeness, and I was afraid that seeing their day-to-day life together might blow up in my face. I had no choice but to admit that Abby, Judith, and Jack were right—even if they didn't come out and say it: we needed to sort out our problems once and for all to truly move on. We had to end a relationship that had never had the chance to begin, and never would.

While I was going up to their cottage, I received a text from Olivier: "Enjoy your last night in Ireland. See you tomorrow. Lots of love."

"Thanks . . . Can't wait to see you. Love," I replied, before knocking on the door.

Declan opened the door, all smiles, wearing his pajamas. He took my hand and led me into the living room; it was hard to make headway as Postman Pat was jumping all over me. The TV was on, the cartoon channel; Edward was behind the counter in the kitchen, making dinner. He glanced over at me; impossible to judge his state of mind.

"Did you say goodbye to the beach?"

"Yes . . ."

"Diane, are you coming?"

Declan kept pulling my arm.

"Yes, just give me two minutes."

He shrugged his shoulders and jumped onto the couch with his dog. I sat down at the counter, opposite Edward.

"You didn't have to invite me tonight."

"Did you ever see me do anything I didn't want to?" he retorted, without looking at me.

"Can I help with anything?"

He stared into my eyes.

"Read a story to Declan while I finish making dinner?"

"It would be better to swap jobs; that would be better for both of you."

"You're not going to do the cooking. Really!"

"None of that . . . politeness doesn't suit us."

I went behind the counter, took the wooden spoon from him, and pushed him into the living room. He shook his head before picking up a book from his son's schoolbag. Declan tried to squirm out of it but his father's expression convinced him not to insist. Lulled by the mixture of his little voice and his father's hoarse one, I finished the cooking and set the table. Edward took his time to make sure that Declan understood everything; his patience took my breath away. When the meal was ready, I walked past without interrupting them and went outside for a smoke. Two minutes later, the bay window opened and Edward joined me, smoking a cigarette.

"I had to promise him he could sit next to you at the table; I hope you won't be angry with me."

"No problem."

The conversation stopped there. All we could hear was the sound of cigarettes being smoked through the wind and the waves. It was still too early to open the floodgates. In any case, Declan wouldn't leave us any time to relax. He came out to find us, his stomach growling.

Once we started to eat, he made sure there was conversation; he talked nonstop about what happened with his friends at school before asking me a direct question.

"You're leaving tomorrow? Is that really true?"

"Yes, I'm taking a plane."

"Why? It isn't fair . . . "

"I was here on vacation; I live in Paris. I work there. Remember?"

"Yes . . . Daddy, could we go and visit Diane sometime?"

"We'll see."

"But we could go when I'm off school!"

Edward's face clouded over.

"Declan," I said, "You have all the time in the world to come and see me. OK?"

He grumbled, finished his yoghurt and went to throw the empty pot in the garbage, without saying a word. Then he sat down on the couch, sulking. Edward watched him, tense and worried. He got up from the table and sat down opposite his son. He stroked his hair.

"You remember that Abby's sick, don't you, and that we have to take care of her and help Jack. That's why I can't take you to Paris to see Diane."

"But *you* went . . . "

"That's true, but I shouldn't have . . . "

Declan lowered his head; Edward took a deep breath.

"Now it's time to go to bed."

"No, daddy! I don't want to!"

Anguish ran through him and showed on his unhappy face.

"You have no choice. You have school tomorrow."

"Please, daddy! I want to stay with you and Diane."

"No. Go and say goodbye to Diane."

He leapt off the couch and crushed himself against me, holding onto my waist and crying. I took a deep breath. Edward stared at me, distraught, before putting his head in his hands.

"Diane, I don't want to go to bed, I don't want to, don't want to . . . "

"Listen, daddy is right. You have to go to bed."

"No," he sobbed.

I looked at Edward; there was nothing he could do; he had no strength left. They needed some help, and I was there . . .

"Do you want me to come with you, like the other night?"

He held me even tighter: his answer was clear.

"Come on."

He headed toward the stairs without looking at his father.

"Aren't you forgetting something!" I reminded him.

He turned around and ran into Edward's arms. I left them alone and went up to his room. I could hear his little footsteps on the stairs, then listened to him brush his teeth. While he was doing that, I turned on the beside lamp, straightened out his bed, which hadn't been made, and got his mother's scarf that was hidden under the mattress. He came into his room and slipped under the covers. I knelt down beside his bed and stroked his forehead and face.

"Declan, daddy is doing everything he can for you . . . he knows how much you're hurting . . . you have to help him; what I'm asking of you is complicated . . . but you have to let him sleep in his own bed. You're a brave little boy . . . your daddy won't ever leave you . . . When you're asleep, he's always home . . . Can you promise me you'll try?"

He nodded.

"Do you want me to sing you the lullaby?"

"When will you come back?"

I tilted my head to one side and smiled.

"I don't know . . . I can't promise anything."

"Will we see each other again?"

"Someday . . . Now go to sleep."

I sang the lullaby several times while continuing to stroke his hair. His little eyes fought for a while before closing. He was also exhausted. When I felt he was calm, I kissed his forehead and stood up. Before closing the door, I looked at him one last time and sighed.

In the living room, everything had been cleared away, the bay window was open, and there was a fire in the fireplace. Edward was standing near the window sill, smoking a cigarette and looking extremely nervous.

"He's asleep," I whispered. "I tried to make him understand that you also had to sleep in your own bed."

He closed his eyes.

"I could never thank you enough."

"It's not necessary . . . but if you have any Guinness in the fridge, I wouldn't say no. I'd gladly have a last one before going back to Paris."

"Can't you get it in France?"

"I'm sure it wouldn't taste the same as it does here."

A few minutes later, he was handing me a pint. We didn't clink glasses. Standing near the fireplace, I lit a cigarette. I made sure not to look at him even though I could feel him staring at me. I noticed an album on one of the bookshelves. Curiosity got the better of me.

"Is this your portfolio?"

"That's right."

"May I?"

"If you'd like."

I threw my cigarette into the fire, put my glass down on the coffee table, picked up the thing I wanted to see, and settled down in an armchair opposite him.

I started leafing through the album with the greatest care. The first photographs left me stunned.

"Are these the Aran Islands at the front?"

"You have a good memory."

My stomach knotted when I recognized myself in one of the shots.

"How could I forget?" I said very softly.

I continued looking through the album. His mood was palpable in every frame. I had the impression that he was telling a story with his portfolio, a romance told in pictures in the literal meaning of the term. The beginning was full of light and air, you could breathe in the landscapes he showed us. But then, the atmosphere became more oppressive: the sky was always dark, blotted out by threatening clouds; the sea was raging, the boats swaying in a storm. And then, gradually, it was as if you could breathe again, a ray of sun reflected off the sea before lighting up the sky. The last photo was a shadow of a child running along the beach, the waves licking the feet of the subject, or Declan, I should say. Edward's portfolio told his story, what he'd been through the past few months, as if he'd tried to exorcise his ordeal, to turn the page through his photos. Completely absorbed in my "reading," I hadn't noticed he'd stood up and was standing by the fireplace with his back to me. I put the portfolio back on the shelf and drank my Guinness to regain control of my emotions. It took all my courage to walk over to him.

"Edward . . . I'm sorry to have gone like that, so suddenly. It was wrong to do that to you. I'm sorry . . . "

He turned around and looked deep into my eyes.

"You shouldn't regret anything," he said harshly. "It's good that you met my son; you know my priorities now. You've built a new life for yourself with Olivier, and I'm happy for you."

His voice faltered slightly; I could feel a lump in my throat. He looked at me even more intensely.

"You made the right decision at the time," he continued, his voice softer. "Declan is here . . . we didn't have a future together."

He was right about everything: we would have ended up breaking up. Several seconds passed while we stood dead still. I breathed in deeply.

"It's late; I'm going to go now; it's for the best."

"We've said everything we had to."

"Yes . . . I think so."

He followed me to the entrance hall.

"I'll walk you to your car."

"If you'd like."

We were hit by a gust of wind; it was pitch black out. I opened the car door and threw my bag onto the passenger seat.

"Judith and I will keep you informed about Abby."

"Thank you . . . take care of yourself, Edward."

"I'll try . . ."

I got into the car without saying any more. We looked at each other one last time: it was over. He lit a cigarette and waited until I'd driven off before going back inside.

Abby and Jack were asleep when I got back. I went up to my room, quietly packed my suitcase and went to bed, knowing very well that sleep would not come easily. Relief and sadness alternated, battling for prime place in my emotions. The situation between Edward and me was now clear: I'd cut my ties to him. The joy of going back to Olivier made up for my feeling of incompleteness. My relationship with Edward didn't exist any more. I finally fell asleep.

Waking up was difficult; depression hit me as soon as I opened my eyes. After showering and getting dressed, I stripped the sheets from the bed and put them in the washing machine. Once my room was clean, I went downstairs, carrying my large suitcase. Abby greeted me with a big smile and an enormous breakfast. I was going to make an effort for her; if worst came to worst, I'd throw up on the road. I kissed her on both cheeks.

"Did you have a good evening?" I asked her.

"Of course. And what about you, with Edward and Declan?"

"It was very nice."

"You don't want to talk about it?"

"There's not much to say . . . "

"She understands," Jack broke in, "Don't you Abby?"

"Come along then; you need your strength for the journey," she said, taking me by the arm.

Even though we tried to be cheerful during our last meal together, we failed.

"Do you need anything for the trip? Something to eat or drink?"

"Thanks, Abby, but no . . . I'll get going . . . the longer we put it off, the worse it will be . . . "

Jack was the first to stand up. He took my bags and went outside. Abby and I looked at each other.

"Will you help me, my darling?"

I hurried to the other side of the table to take her arm. She stroked my hand as we walked. I held back my tears. The car arrived too quickly. Jack came over to me and opened his arms.

"My little Frenchwoman," he sighed, hugging me tight. "Take good care of yourself."

"I promise," I replied, sniffling.

"The car's waiting for you."

He let go of me, pulled an enormous handkerchief out of his pocket, and wiped his eyes and nose. I turned toward Abby, who stroked my cheek.

"We've said everything we had to, my little one."

I nodded, incapable of uttering a sound.

"Promise me one last thing: don't be sad when I'm gone, don't cry. Make sure our reunion was a good one; we had time together to prepare ourselves."

I looked up to the heavens before drying my eyes and taking a deep breath.

"Don't make me lie when I tell your Colin and Clara that you're fine, and happy, and that they can be proud of you. All right?"

As a promise and to say goodbye, I hugged her tightly in my arms and whispered in her ear that I loved her like a mother. She stroked my cheek, tears in her eyes, before letting go of me. I climbed into the car without looking at them and drove off without looking back. I drove about 12 kilometers before stopping on the shoulder of the road to cry my heart out.

It's a miracle that I managed to make it to Dublin airport without causing an accident. I couldn't stop crying for the entire four hours it took to get there; I was still crying when I returned the rental car, while checking in my bags, going through security, and sending a text to Olivier once I was on the plane. When it took off, I felt like I was being ripped apart, that I was being torn from my home. But I gritted my teeth and tried to calm myself down. The man waiting for me in Paris didn't deserve to see me in this state. In order to compose myself and look as calm as possible, or rather, make my face look less swollen, I got off after most of the other passengers and stopped in the restroom to splash cold water on my face and touch up my makeup before getting my suitcase from the conveyor belt. The doors from Customs opened; he was there, smiling, calmly waiting to meet me. I ran and threw myself into his arms, not because I thought I should or to pretend to be happy, but because I really wanted him to hold me. The pain of having left Mulranny was still with me, it would always be with me, I knew that, but I could breathe a bit easier with Olivier by my side.

8

Life continued as before from the next morning. I'd slept at Olivier's place and our night had made me feel much better. He took me home and carried my suitcase upstairs while I went into the bookstore. I didn't have to tell him I wanted to be alone; he'd understood that by himself. First bit of luck: everything was intact. Felix hadn't ransacked anything while I was away and it was clean. He must have really taken responsibility and would doubtlessly demand a few days off, or a bonus! Second bit of luck, and the most important one: I felt good here, and I was excited at the idea of getting back to work. My trip to Ireland hadn't broken my ties to the bookstore. Olivier knocked on the back door and I went and opened it.

"Thank you," I said, then kissed him. "Do you have time to have a coffee with me?"

"Do you really have to ask!"

We sat down at the counter, next to each other. Olivier turned my head to him, stroked my cheek and took one of my hands in his.

"Are you all right?"

"Yes, promise."

"You don't regret anything then?"

"Not for a second."

"That's good . . . and the little boy?"

"Oh . . . Declan . . . I managed, and better than I thought I would."

"Maybe because you know his father."

"And his whole family . . . I don't know . . . he's sweet . . . And, well . . . he's going to suffer more. Abby has become his grandmother . . . when she goes . . . "

My voice faltered.

"Don't think about that."

"You're right."

"The main thing is that you got back in contact with your friends. It's up to you to keep in touch now."

He finished his coffee and was getting ready to go.

"I have no other choice now!"

I clung onto him and walked him out to the street.

"Do you want to see a movie tonight?" he suggested.

"Why not! But let's sleep at my place."

"OK."

He kissed me and headed for his office.

As I suspected, Felix took part of the day off. He took his time and arrived around three o'clock.

"The owner is chasing the customers away! There were more people here when I was behind the counter."

"Happy to see you too, Felix!"

He planted a kiss on my cheek, helped himself to a coffee, and leaned on the counter, watching me.

"What are you doing?" I asked.

"Taking stock . . . "

"And your verdict?"

"Superficially, you pass the first test. You must have cried so much yesterday that you slept like a log. Which is why you now look fresh as a daisy instead of having puffy eyes. But inside, on the other hand . . . less sure that everything is working properly . . . "

"It's true; I won't pretend it wasn't painfully difficult to say goodbye to Abby. I'll never see her again . . . can you understand that?"

He nodded.

"As for the rest, I'm in fine shape. I got some fresh air and had a great time with Judith. All in all, everything made me happy!"

"And Edward?"

"What about Edward? He's doing the best he can. We settled everything once and for all. It was the best thing to do."

"You mean that you didn't succumb to his gruff, wild charm a second time!"

"Felix, he's a father now."

"Exactly. I'd really like to become a nanny; he must be incredibly sexy with his kid!"

I raised my eyes to heaven.

"You're forgetting one little detail: I have Olivier; I love Olivier."

"Good point. Now I feel reassured!"

During the weeks that followed, the humdrum routine of daily life continued; Happy People lived up to my highest expectations, Felix was in top form, and I felt good with Olivier. One more thing: I spoke to Abby and Judith on the phone once a week. And that filled me with joy, as if I were closing a gap inside me.

We were slouched in front of the television, at Olivier's place. I was dozing in his arms, totally uninterested in the film he found captivating.

"Go to bed," he finally said to me.

"Won't that bother you?"

"Don't be silly!"

I gave him a kiss on the neck and made a quick stop in the bathroom before climbing into bed. I wasn't completely asleep when Olivier slipped under the covers and pulled me close.

"Didn't you watch the end?"

"I already knew what happened. Did you set the alarm?"

"Shit!"

"What?"

"I forgot my bag again; it's under the counter at the bookstore. I'll have to stop at my place to change clothes before opening up."

I grabbed my phone from the night table and set the alarm for twenty minutes earlier. I was still moaning about it when I got back in bed.

"Diane?"

"Yes."

"Maybe we could look for an apartment?"

"You want us to live together?"

"You could put it that way! Listen, we spend every night together and we're past the age of emptying out a drawer for each other."

"You know that it's usually the woman who asks?"

"Then it's my feminine side expressing itself! What do you think?"

"Maybe you're right . . . "

Why put off this next step? He leaned over me, genuinely surprised, a big smile on his face. I was making him happy . . .

"Do you mean it? You want to live with me?"

"Yes!"

He kissed me, then leaned his head against mine. He was so considerate of me that I always had the feeling I was his fragile little thing.

"I would have understood if you weren't ready . . . we'll choose a place that's ours."

"That will be nice . . . "

A few days later, Olivier was in the bookstore; he was leafing through the private ads while calling the real estate agents in the neighborhood. He underlined things, made lists, got annoyed at the ridiculous ads and excited when he managed to get us a viewing. It was an arduous task; he'd gotten it into his head to find us an apartment in the area . . . For me, to make things easy for me.

"We have a problem!" he said.

"What's that?"

"All the viewings are next Saturday."

"Ah . . . "

"Indeed."

We both had the same instinctive idea: to look at Felix who was eating one piece of candy after another. He'd started his "stop smoking" plan without intending to do without cigarettes. "I'm preparing myself, getting in practice," he told me, very convinced. When he noticed we were both staring at him, he raised one eyebrow and popped a piece of candy in his mouth.

"What exactly are you two plotting?"

"You have to do Diane a favor."

"That will cost you . . . "

"Felix, please," I insisted. "We have apartments to visit on Saturday."

"No problem! Take all the time you need to choose your love nest! As long as she leaves her hovel! And I'm splitting now!"

He wolfed down one last piece of candy before going over to Olivier and giving him a big hug.

"If you weren't around, I don't know what would have happened to me with her hanging on!"

"Ha! That's enough!" I said, annoyed.

"I love you, Diane!"

He skipped away.

"We have to find a place where we'll be happy," I said to Olivier.

"I hope so! Are you really sure?"

"Yes!"

"You won't miss living here?"

"Of course I will . . . but I want to move forward with you."

I leaned over the counter and kissed him. I had to continue taking the next step, even if I sometimes told myself that we were going too fast; perhaps I had agreed to it because it felt comfortable and easy, or because I wanted things to remain simple, without any conflict, and so I wouldn't be going backwards. That was something I refused to allow myself to do. I was content with Olivier; everything was gentle and peaceful.

When he arrived the next evening, I was about to call Abby. He came behind the counter to kiss me.

"Did you have a good day?" I asked him.

"Very good. Are you closing up soon?"

"First I want to call Abby."

"Of course.

"Help yourself to a beer."

I didn't hide when I was calling Ireland. He knew how much I cared about Abby and needed to talk to her. He didn't take offence. I sat down near the cash register and leaned on the counter. Olivier sat down on the other side and was leafing through a magazine. I dialed Abby and Jack's number; I knew it by heart. It took a long time for someone to answer— it seemed interminable to me.

"Yes!"

It was neither Abby nor Jack. A shudder ran down my spine.

"Edward . . . it's Diane."

Out of the corner of my eye, I saw Olivier look up slightly from his magazine.

"How are you?" he asked after a long silence.

"Oh . . . good, and you?"

"I'm OK . . . "

I could hear Declan's voice behind him and smiled.

"And your son?"

"Better . . . in fact . . . I'm teaching him some photography . . . "

"Really? That's wonderful . . . I . . . "

I preferred to stop talking rather than admitting out loud that I'd love to see the two of them with their cameras. That urge came from the past and I was surprised at how very strong it was . . .

"Who is it, daddy?"

Edward sighed into the receiver.

"Diane."

"I want to talk to her! Diane! Diane!"

"Edward, tell him I send him my love but I'm in a hurry. Is Abby there?"

A simple precaution: in reality, I had all the time in the world.

"She's gone to bed, but I'll put Jack on. See you soon."

While talking to Jack, I could hear Edward calming Declan down; he couldn't understand why he was the only one who didn't get to talk to me.

His father explained that I was in a hurry and I was with my family in Paris. That kept a distance and everything in its proper place. I stopped listening to them and concentrated on the news. Jack told me that Abby had been very tired for several days. I could sense the anxiety in his voice, but also his resignation.

"I'll tell her you called; she'll give me what for because I didn't wake her up! Your calls always do her a lot of good."

"I'll try again tomorrow. Give her a kiss from me. And a big hug to you, Jack."

"And to you, my little Frenchwoman."

I hung up. For the first time since I returned, just over a month ago, I wanted to be somewhere else. I wanted to watch over Abby.

"Diane?"

"She was sleeping; she doesn't sound in good shape."

I sighed.

"I'll call back tomorrow; maybe I'll have more luck . . . Tell me about the apartments; that will keep my mind off it!"

The next day, while I was talking to Abby, I had a bad feeling. Of course, she wasn't as weak as I'd imagined, but she spent a long time giving me a lot of advice—"Let time do its work, smile, don't cry, listen to your heart"—calling me "her little girl" with every sentence, in a voice full of love and affection.

Saturday came quickly. The marathon of viewings started early and left me exhausted. We saw the worst places and the best. Olivier had taken charge of our file; all I'd done was provide him with various documents for my part of the deal. He took care to sell us to the owners while I strolled around our potential future home. He really fell in love with an apartment in the Temple district, and it was nice seeing him so enthusiastic. There was nothing to be said; it was perfect: two-bedrooms with a small balcony and a wonderful view, a little kitchen and a newly renovated bathroom with an Italian shower. And to Olivier's immense delight, it was available immediately. He took my arm and led me to a corner of the living room.

"What do you think?"

"This would be a good place for us."

"It's not too far from the bookstore?"

"Really! I can walk for ten minutes!"

I could see the doubt on his face. I took the file from him and handed it to the real estate agent.

"When do you think you'll be able to give us an answer from the owner?"

"Next week."

"Fine. We'll wait for your call."

I took Olivier's hand, glanced one last time around the living room and walked us to the elevator.

"You see? Done!"

I hugged him with all my heart, but also to silence a feeling of anguish I could sense building up in me. We slowly walked back to Happy People, holding hands, talking about moving, like a normal couple. When he got to the bookstore, Olivier got a call from a friend, so stayed outside on the sidewalk to talk to him. Before putting myself through Felix's interrogation, I poured myself a coffee.

"We made an offer to rent an apartment; we should know if it's been accepted soon."

"Wow! I don't believe it. You're going through with it!"

"Yep!"

He stared at me.

"Are you happy?"

"It's just a little strange. I'm going to live with a man who isn't Colin."

"That's true, but you love him."

"Right."

When Olivier joined us, he had a big smile on his face; he kissed me and I told myself that I had to stop torturing myself with a thousand questions: I was ready for him. I'd finally found peace.

I said the same thing to myself again that evening. We were invited to have dinner at his friend's house—the young couple with the baby. Her babbling set my nerves on edge the second we got there. I found this picture-perfect little family unbearable, and I knew why. It made me think back to my family with Colin and Clara. They were so carefree, happy as could be, not thinking for a single second that everything could fall apart. Life had arranged for me to meet a man who had never been a father and was not concerned about passing on his heritage. I had everything I needed. And yet, I realized that I preferred the company of people who had been battered by life—that was what moved me, stimulated me.

When the baby was asleep, I could relax and enjoy the evening without brooding. At least I was with parents who didn't hold their child in their arms the entire time. Olivier was the one who told them our big news. They didn't hide their joy, and we made a toast to our apartment. Then they offered to help us move. Olivier got teased: moving twice in less than two months, that was really too much! I promised to buy everyone drinks as a reward. I was starting to get nervous; Olivier noticed and leaned towards me.

"Go and have a cigarette, no one will mind."

"Thanks . . . "

I grabbed my ciggies and phone from my bag and excused myself. I had to go down to the street to get my dose of nicotine. Judith had tried to call me. She answered at the first ring.

"So what are you doing with your Saturday night?"

"I'm having dinner with some of Olivier's friends. We're celebrating our new apartment!"

"What? You're going to live with him! So it's really serious?"

"So it seems . . . And what about you, where are you going tonight?"

"Where do you think?"

I laughed.

"I'm at Temple Bar, out on the town tonight," she said, confirming my suspicions.

"Good, so everything's all right?"

"Yes, Abby's been tired recently but she's fine now. A scare over nothing."

"You're right to enjoy yourself. Have a Guinness for me!"

"Not just one, trust me. Many!"

As she was hanging up, I heard her order a pint amid the noise of happy people in the pub. That made me want to be there. I went back upstairs and took my place at the dinner table.

We got the apartment. We had to sign the lease the following week and pick up the keys shortly after. I was caught
up in a whirlwind; I followed Olivier, who continued to do
everything necessary. He managed to condense several days
into one, juggling his patients' appointments, our official documents, and arrangements for the move, while all I did was
spend time at the bookstore. You'd think that my workload
had doubled: I constantly thought about the bookstore, spent
every night there, staying a little later each day. Was I taking
refuge there to avoid my real problems? Happy People was
where I felt at home, the place where I could find a balance
again. I carefully avoided any conversations with Felix. He
had a knack for putting his finger exactly where it hurt. Any
doubt was forbidden.

That Monday, we spent the whole evening packing boxes
at Olivier's place. Preparing for the move after work had one
advantage: it didn't give me time to think any further about
the commitment I was making to him. It was obvious I didn't
have his enthusiasm or eagerness at the idea of living together.
Waves of memories surged up: I had been so excited to move
in with Colin; it was all I thought about at the time; I was
obsessed. And yet, I was sure I now loved Olivier enough to
see it through. I had to accept that I'd grown up, that love at
twenty-five couldn't compare with love at thirty-five, especially when you've once had a family.

Both of us collapsed like a log when we went to bed. But
our sleep was disturbed by my cell phone ringing in the middle of the night. I felt around for it on the night table. Despite my eyes being half closed, I saw "Judith" on the screen

and knew. When I answered, I could hear the tears in her voice.

"Diane . . . it's over . . . "

"My poor Judith . . . "

I listened as she told me that Abby hadn't suffered, she'd smiled right up to the end and had gone to sleep peacefully in Jack's arms two days earlier. He had instructions from her for all of us.

Judith, Edward, Declan, and me. Hearing that I'd been in Abby's thoughts at the end made me shed my first tears.

"I'm so sorry to call you so late, but this is the first chance I've had. We've been getting everything ready . . . "

"Don't worry. Where are you?"

"At their place; I don't want to leave Jack alone. And Edward is taking care of Declan."

"Try to get some sleep; I'll call you tomorrow. I want to be with you . . . "

"I know . . . we all miss you . . . "

She hung up. I sat down on the bed and started sobbing. Olivier took me in his arms to calm me down; I was shaking. I had expected to lose Abby; I knew she was dying. But it hurt to think she would no longer keep her little troop in line, that she'd no longer be able to take care of anyone. Jack had lost his other half.

"I'm so sorry," whispered Olivier. "What can I do to help you?"

"Nothing."

He kissed me on the forehead, rocked me in his arms, and yet, I still felt alone; here was not where I wanted to be.

"I have to call Edward."

I disentangled myself from Olivier, got out of bed, threw on a sweater, and went into the living room while dialing Edward's number. He picked up at the first ring.

"Diane," he whispered into the phone, "I was hoping you'd call."

I needed to hear your voice, I thought.

"I'm here . . . "

I could hear the sound of his lighter and the first drag on his cigarette. I lit one, too. Each of us was smoking a cigarette in his own country, but together. I could hear the wind blowing.

"Where are you?"

"On the porch."

"And Declan?"

"He just fell asleep."

"When is the funeral?"

"The day after tomorrow."

"So soon!"

"Jack doesn't want to drag things out . . . he's ready."

"I'm going to come."

"You can't drop everything to be with us, even if I want . . . "

"My place is with you all and no one is going to stop me from coming."

"Thank you . . . Declan woke up; he's crying."

"Call me when he's back asleep, it doesn't matter what time, I'll answer. I have to book a plane ticket."

"Diane, I . . . "

"Go to your son."

I hung up, then stared at my phone for a long time before realizing that Olivier had come into the room. He'd been thoughtful enough to bring me an ashtray. I hadn't even noticed him.

"Can I borrow your computer?"

"What are you going to do?"

"I have to get a plane ticket for tomorrow."

"What?!"

"My place is at Abby's funeral. I'd never forgive myself if I didn't go."

"I understand."

He went and got his computer and sat down next to me on the couch.

"Go to bed."

"Diane, let me do something for you."

I put my arms around his neck. I was so sorry to do this to him, to spoil his plans, but I felt I was being called. My life had just been disrupted. And nothing, not the bookstore, not Olivier, not Felix, nothing could fight this urge.

"You can't do anything; I'm really sorry. Don't stay up all night because of me."

He nodded, kissed me, and stood up.

"I won't go to sleep without you, but I'll leave you alone, if that's what you want."

"Forgive me."

He didn't reply. I watched him as he walked back to the bedroom, leaving the door open. While I was looking for a flight, all I could think about was Edward, who must be fighting Declan's nightmares. I had just paid for my tickets when the phone rang.

"Edward . . . "

"He's asleep now."

"You should do the same."

"And you!"

I smiled.

"I have my ticket; I'll get there at eight o'clock tomorrow night and drive over right away."

"That's not a good idea. I'll pick you up."

"Don't be silly. I've always hired a car, it's what I usually do. I can manage like a grown-up. If there's one person in the world who never tried to overprotect me, it's you, so don't start now!"

"No argument. I'm picking you up."

"You won't be driving during the day. What about Declan? He'll be terrified to see you go."

"If I tell him I'm going to get you, he'll let me go . . . Judith will be with him, and it will do her good to be away from Abby for a few hours. I'll leave late afternoon and we'll be back by midnight."

"You're being ridiculous."

"Please, Diane. Let me come and get you; I need to get some air, to breathe."

His call for help left me reeling.

"All right . . . go to sleep now."

"See you tomorrow."

He hung up. I took the time to smoke a cigarette; I needed one to realize I was actually leaving the next day for Mulranny to go to Abby's funeral. And yet, deep down, I'd always known that I'd go back there when it happened. Ready to put myself in a dangerous position. My body was still in Paris but my spirit was already over there. When I went back into the bedroom, I couldn't help noticing that Olivier wasn't asleep; he was waiting for me, one arm folded under his head. He pulled back the covers for me; I slipped under them and pressed myself against him; he held me tight.

"How long will you be gone?"

"Three days. Don't worry, we'll move in on time."

"That's not what I'm worried about . . . ".

"What is it then?"

"It's you."

"Don't worry, I'm not going to fall apart. Abby's death has nothing to do with what happened to me; I was prepared for this. And I hope to keep my promise to her not to cry and to get on with my life.

"Really?"

I didn't answer. He held me tight all night long. Sleep finally came and I managed to get a few hours. When I opened my eyes, realizing I'd lost Abby hit me and took my breath away for a moment. I controlled myself, fighting the pain. I had to get on with my day, prepare for being away, and reassure Olivier, whose expression of anxiety had only got worse during the night. He never took his eyes off me while we were having breakfast.

"What time does your plane leave tonight?"

"Seven o'clock."

"I'll sort things out so I can take you."

"Don't cancel any patients because of me."

"I insist, so don't try to stop me."

Half an hour later, he left me at the bookstore. I opened the café and immediately got busy, instead of chatting with my early customers, as I usually did; I got everything in order, made sure that Felix would want for nothing and made time to call Judith. She sounded better than the night before; Edward had told her I was coming, and I could sense she was relieved. Then she put Jack on, even though I wasn't prepared to talk to him.

"How are you, my little Frenchwoman?"

"Never mind about me, how are you?"

"Everything's all right. We had our time together. I have a message for you, but you already know what it is."

"Yes," I said, sniffling.

"I'm touched that you're making the trip. You'll feel better for it, you'll see."

"See you tomorrow, Jack."

My shoulders drooped as I hung up.

"What does that mean: see you tomorrow, Jack?"

I jumped when I heard Felix.

"I'm getting a plane tonight. Abby died."

I turned my back to him and poured myself a coffee.

"You can't do that! You can't go to a funeral in Ireland."

He grabbed me by the shoulders and forced me to look at him.

"Nothing's stopping me!"

"Everything should be stopping you! Shit! Your life is going well, you have Olivier, the bookstore, you've turned the
page. Forget Ireland and everyone there!"

"Don't ask me to do the impossible! And don't make such
a fuss; I'll be gone for three days and back in time to move."

"In what state?"

"I've had enough of everyone worrying about me—you,
Olivier. Stop thinking I'm going to fall apart at the first hur-
dle. I'm not the same now, I've taken control of my life, I'm
fine and I know what I want. And what I want, what my heart
is telling me, is to go and say goodbye to Abby, and to be at
the side of the people I love."

"And the kid, is he one of the people you love?"

His attack made me jump and stammer.

"I don't know . . . Declan is . . . "

"Edward's son! That's what he is!"

I looked down at my feet. Felix held me tightly against
him.

"You're a pain in the ass, Diane. Go and screw up your
head. I'll be here to pick up the pieces."

"There won't be any pieces to pick up."

"Stop playing the fool. It really doesn't suit you."

The day passed by very quickly; I barely ate breakfast so I
could pack my suitcase. Felix agreed to work for the three
days I was away. Olivier took me to the airport, as he'd said
he would. All Felix did when we said goodbye was to kiss me
on both cheeks and give me a look that meant "Be careful." I
left the bookstore, held Olivier's hand, and stopped in the
street after taking three steps to take a final look at my book

café. I glanced at the display, the sign . . . Once again, I was leaving my refuge . . . for them, for Ireland . . .

The train journey took place in silence. Olivier held me close, kissed my hair now and again, and stroked my hands. I was responsible for his sadness, and I didn't like that feeling. Was selfishness becoming second nature to me? I'd made this decision without thinking about him, or how it might affect him, without considering asking his advice for a single second.

I'd just checked in and we were outside; I was smoking one last cigarette before boarding when my phone rang.

"Yes, Edward."

Olivier held me even closer.

"I'm on the road and wanted to know if your flight was on time."

"That's what's posted."

"I'll meet you when you get through Customs."

"That's great. I'll get off the plane as fast as I can."

"See you soon."

He hung up before I could reply. I turned toward Olivier who hadn't taken his eyes off me; he was still anxious.

"Are you mad at me?"

"Of course not . . . They're like family to you . . . It's just not completely clear why you're closing the door on that part of your life to me. I can't take care of you the way I'd like to, that's all."

I took his hands in mine.

"When I get back, we'll be together. Don't worry."

"Do you still want to move next weekend?"

"Yes!"

He took me in his arms and sighed into my neck.

"You'd better go now."

He walked me as far as the last security gate.

"Don't wait until you can't see me any more before going home, OK? And please, don't rearrange your schedule to come and meet me when I get back."

He agreed and kissed me. I could feel he put all his love in that kiss, all his sweetness and tenderness. I returned his kiss as best I could. But I couldn't tell how much I believed in it myself.

9

I was the first passenger to undo my seatbelt when the plane stopped on the tarmac, and the first out of the cabin. And I was the only one to loudly shout "Shit!" when I realized I had to walk through the entire airport. The wheels on my suitcase sometimes flew into the air, that's how fast I was running. The sound it made aroused the curiosity of the other passengers, who immediately made way for me to pass. I refused to accept the reason I was running like that. The doors finally opened; Edward was waiting for me on the other side, leaning against a wall, an unlit cigarette between his lips. I slowed down to a stop; he stood up straight and walked toward me. I met him halfway, silencing what my heart was telling me. When we were standing face to face, he looked deep into my eyes.

"Shall we go?" he asked, out of politeness, taking my bag from me.

"Yes."

He stepped closer and never took his eyes off me. Then he kissed me on the forehead; I held my breath and closed my eyes. When he walked away, headed for the parking lot, it took me a few seconds to come down to earth before follow- ing him. A blast of cold hit me. Winter had come with its biting wind and icy drops of rain. That should have made me think straight. Edward lit a cigarette and handed me the pack as we walked, glancing at me over his shoulder. I forbid my- self from reacting as his fingers lightly brushed against mine. We didn't lose any time, setting off as soon as my suitcase was in the trunk, without saying a word to each other. Driving along in the pitch darkness was so exhilarating that I thought Felix might be right: I was going to get all confused, in spite of the purpose of my trip. At certain moments, I felt almost innocent. I stared at Edward; he drove fast, with one hand on the steering wheel, sure of himself, lost in thought. He must have sensed I was watching him; he looked away from the road and stared deep into my eyes. What was happening was impossible, forbidden. What had happened to the distance between us of just a few weeks earlier? We both started breathing again at the same moment. The sound of my phone ringing took him back to concentrating on driving. I cleared my throat before answering.

"Olivier, I was about to call you! We're on our way."

"That's good. Everything OK?"

"Yes."

"I won't keep you any longer. Send my condolences to Edward."

"I will. Big kiss."

"Diane . . . I love you."

"Me too."

I felt bad saying those two little words. I closed my eyes as I hung up and squeezed my phone in my hand as hard as I could. Edward lit a cigarette; so did I. I stared at the road through my window.

"Olivier sends you his condolences."

"Thank him for me . . . Judith told me you were living with him."

"We're moving in together in four days."

Silence and reality hit us hard. I slumped down in my seat, exhausted by my contradictory emotions. After about an hour, Edward pulled off the highway at a rest stop.

"I need some coffee. No point in asking if you'd like one . . . "

He got out of the car and pulled up the collar of his pea jacket. I followed him a few moments later and found him in front of the coffee machines. He gave a big yawn and ran his hand through his hair. He handed me a coffee while his cup was being filled.

"Ready to go?" he asked, after picking up his coffee.

He didn't wait for me to answer. Once outside, he raised his face to the rain. He couldn't keep going like this.

"How many days has it been since you've slept?"

"Three, I'm with Declan every night."

"Give me the keys, have a nap while I drive. No arguments; I know the way, I know how to drive on the left, and you need to rest."

He took a drink of coffee before shaking his head and handing me the keys. We both started laughing hard, and nervously, when we got into the car; I was miles away from the steering wheel. When I'd adjusted everything to my size, I started the engine and turned toward him.

"Go to sleep now."

He put some music on: Alt-J's latest album, and relaxed back in his seat. He raised his hand, reaching toward my cheek, but went no further. I put the car in first gear; he hadn't stopped looking at me. A few minutes after we got back onto the highway, he whispered: "Diane . . . thank you."

I glanced over at him, he was turned towards me, sleeping. For the first time, I felt like I was protecting him, taking care of him. I wished we could drive forever, without stopping, so he could finally truly rest, so I could continue to feel he was at peace; his face looked so relaxed. His snoring made me smile and told me he was in a deep sleep. That was already better than nothing for him. For me, it was two hours of thinking. Driving always had that effect on me. And that couldn't happen in Paris! Driving, soothed by the music and concentrating on the road, made me feel wrapped in a cocoon. I might as well take advantage of the situation, which forced me to look deep into my soul. I'd believed the problem of Edward had been solved . . . How could I have been so stupid? His place in my life was far more important than I cared to admit. How should I act during the days that followed? Let myself go? Listen to myself? Put up barriers? Protect the life I'd rebuilt from the attack of this man who was sleeping next to me? Unless I preferred to fool myself that all this was only because we were both so fragile because Abby had died . . .

As we drove over the last hill before reaching Mulranny, I still hadn't decided what to do, but I was going to have to wake him up. I softly called his name; he moaned and groaned in his sleep before opening his eyes. His first instinct was to light a cigarette.

"We're here," he said, his voice as hoarse as ever.

"Yes."

"You're sleeping at my place."

"What?"

"Abby is at their house; I thought you might not want to sleep in the room next to her."

That would, indeed, have been more than I could bear.

"You can have my room; I'll sleep on the couch, not with Declan."

"Are you sure you don't mind?"

"You're the one I should be asking that. If you prefer, we could find you a room in a Bed and Breakfast."

I'd just parked in front of the cottage.

"Given the late hour, I doubt we'd find a room. And . . . I'd rather stay at your place."

I was putting myself through one hell of a test. Either that or I was listening to my deepest desire . . .

The minute we got inside the house, Judith raced down the stairs.

"He's asleep," she said to her brother.

"I'll go up to him."

He went up three steps at a time, carrying my suitcase, before turning to speak to me.

"Thanks for driving . . . Make yourself at home. Good night!"

I gave him a little smile and he disappeared. I went over to Judith and held her tightly in my arms for several moments.

"How are you feeling?"

"All right, bearing up. And besides, Jack is so strong . . . you'll see tomorrow . . . He's wonderful . . . What about you?"

"I promised Abby I wouldn't break down, so I'm making sure I keep my promise."

"It's good that you're here . . . the whole family is here for her. I have to go; I want to make sure Jack is resting."

She slipped on her coat. Then she looked at me, questioningly, a slight smile on her face.

"And sleeping at my brother's house . . . You're coping?"

"I don't know, Judith . . . I don't know."

She hugged me again and gave me a kiss on each cheek before leaving. The living room was completely dark; I switched off the light in the hall and went upstairs. I saw a ray of light from under the door to Declan's room. Edward had put my suitcase in my room. I'd already slept there once, when I was rock bottom and my relationship with him was at its very worst. That time seemed so far away . . .

After putting on the camisole and leggings I wore as pajamas, I sat down on Edward's bed. I stayed there for a good half an hour before slipping on a sweatshirt and walking over to the closed door. I leaned my head against the wood, then backed away, biting my nails. I did this over and over again several times before deciding to open the door and step out into the hallway. A final stop in front of Declan's room. Then I slowly pushed open the door. Edward was sitting in the armchair, staring at his son. He noticed me. I gestured at him not to move or make a sound. I walked over to Declan's bed. I was filled with secret joy when I saw him; he was sleeping with his fists clenched, tightly holding his mother's scarf. Nothing was stopping me from running my hand through his hair and kissing him on the forehead. I wanted to. My heart was bursting. My kiss tickled him but without waking him up. Then I went and sat down on the floor, next to Edward's chair, legs crossed and my chin resting on my knees. I did what Edward was doing: I was watching over this child. Amidst the sadness over Abby's death, he represented life. A few minutes later, I leaned my head against Edward's leg. Every now and then, he stroked my hair. I lost all sense of time.

After about an hour, perhaps, Edward gently lifted my head, stood up, and took my hand to help me up. He led me out of his son's room and walked me back into his bedroom where the bed awaited me. He stopped at the threshold of the room, still holding my hand.

"Try to get some sleep," he said.

"What about you?"

"I'll stretch out on the couch."

Before letting go of my hand, he came closer and kissed me on the forehead, a kiss that lasted a very long time. Then he raced down the stairs. I closed the door and slipped under the covers. I fell asleep wrapped in his sheets, sheets that still held the scent of him.

I was vaguely starting to wake up when the door opened very noisily.

"Diane! You came back!" shouted Declan, jumping on the bed.

I barely had time to sit up before he threw his arms around my neck.

"I'm sooo happy!"

"Me too, champ."

It was completely true; not a flicker of anguish, no desire to push him away, just a feeling of happiness as I hugged him tight.

"How are you?" I asked.

"All right . . . Come on, we're going downstairs. Daddy made you some coffee."

He tugged at my arm.

"I'll take a shower and come down."

"OK!"

He went out, shouting my message to his father. Seeing him running in his pajamas and bare feet, I stopped myself from asking him to put on some shoes and a sweater.

When I went into the living room twenty minutes later, I had a quite a shock: Edward was wearing a suit and tie. I was dumbfounded; for just a second, I'd forgotten about Abby. Normally, he always looked untidy, his shirt buttoned up wrong and half hanging out of his jeans; now he was wearing a charcoal-grey suit that fit him perfectly, with a tie impeccably done, which gave him even more charisma, as if he needed any more. I must have looked comical because he started to laugh. I walked toward him with difficulty while he poured me a cup of coffee. I took it from him and drank some, without taking my eyes off him. He continued smiling while stroking his beard.

"I wasn't sure if I should shave . . . "

"Don't!"

It sounded like a heartfelt plea.

"It wouldn't be you; she wouldn't have liked that," I continued, knowing I could speak for Abby.

He gave me a little smile and I walked away from him to join Declan and Postman Pat on the couch. Declan snuggled up against me.

"How long are you staying here?"

"Two days."

"Is that all?"

"It's better than nothing . . . "

"I guess," he sighed.

Edward called me and gestured for me to follow him outside. This peaceful moment was coming to an end.

"I have to go to Abby and Jack's; can I leave Declan with you for a couple of hours?"

"Of course; I'll look after him, he has to get dressed. What time is the funeral?"

"Two o'clock. We're having lunch at Abby and Jack's beforehand. Will you come?"

"If it's possible, I'd rather meet you at the church."

"I understand."

Going to a funeral was not going to be easy for me; I needed to be alone to prepare myself. Edward put out his cigarette, went inside to say goodbye to Declan and left.

My time alone with Declan passed quickly; just long enough to get him cleaned up, help him get dressed, and listen to him tell me everything that happened at school in great detail. We were laughing and playing in the living room when Edward got back. His features were more drawn than when he left, his expression serious. He forced himself to smile at his son; I felt for him and more especially, I knew what he'd just gone through: seeing Abby put in the coffin. Our eyes met; I looked up to the heavens to stop myself from crying.

"Is there any coffee left?" he asked.

"Yes."

I got up from the couch and went to join him at the kitchen counter. He was clenching his fists so tightly that you could see his veins standing out: his way of expressing pain. I delicately stroked his hands.

"It will be all right . . . " I whispered.

He gently put his arm around my waist, held me close, sighed, and buried his face in my hair. We were powerless to stop what was happening to us, all our precautions were thrown out the window. The room became strangely silent; I looked around and saw Declan; he was watching us out of the corner of his eye. Edward must have realized it too, for he suddenly let go of me and stepped back.

"Let's go, Declan; Jack and Judith are waiting for us."

"What about Diane? . . . "

"We'll see her at the church."

"Promise?"

"Yes, I'll be there."

He followed his father, glancing back at me over his shoulder. Edward ruffled his hair to get him to look where he was going. The front door slammed shut. I went upstairs to change into an outfit that was more appropriate: a black dress.

Around one o'clock, I forced myself to eat some bread, so I wouldn't pass out. My stomach was in knots, but I wasn't feeling panicky. I went outside to smoke a cigarette, holding my phone. Olivier picked up right away.

"I was waiting for you to call. How's it going?"

"I have to leave for the church very soon; I'm holding up."

I didn't know what else to say to him. An eternity of silence passed between us.

"Do you want me to drop by the bookstore tonight and see how Felix is coping?"

"If you like . . . Have you kept going with the packing?"

"I'm almost finished at my place . . . I could get going on your apartment, to get ahead."

"No, I don't have a lot of stuff . . . "

"I have a patient who's come in; I'll have to go."

"Good luck with work."

"Call me when you can."

"I will . . . take care."

I hung up and breathed again. Being here distanced me from him. Our moving in together was being postponed indefinitely. But that wasn't the most important part. I whistled for Postman Pat, who'd trotted off down the beach, to get him back in the house. When he was lying down, I put on my coat and scarf. No need for an umbrella; the sun had been shining over the cold, blue winter sky for more than an hour.

I walked for about ten minutes to get to the church, which stood in the middle of the cemetery. In the middle of the lawn, in the shadow of a Celtic cross, was the grave where Abby would be put to rest. As the church bells tolled, I felt a kind of insidious fear growing within me. How would I live through this funeral, or rather, survive it? Had I been over-confident about how strong I was? The last funeral I'd been to was for my husband and daughter. It was this fear that made me go inside by a little side door and sit discreetly at the back of the church.

The whole village was there, as well as a group of Judith's friends whom I recognized from New Year's Eve. I could make out Jack, Edward, Declan, and Judith. Like her brother, she'd made a real effort with her outfit. For the first time, she seemed fragile; very thin in her dark grey pinafore dress, wrapped in a black shawl, her lion's mane pulled back into a simple ponytail. I wanted to go to her and hold her close to comfort her, but I didn't let myself. Abby was already there, her coffin covered in flowers. Looking at it, I didn't have the impression of having a wooden box in front of me. I felt her here with us. I noticed Jack out of the corner of my eye; he was walking all the way to the back of the church toward me.

"What are you doing there, hiding, all alone? Abby wouldn't like that. Come on."

He put large, strong arm around my shoulders and led me up the knave, holding me, to seat me in the first row. Judith threw her arms around my neck, crying her heart out. I finally broke down . . . which took a great weight off of me.

"She's going to scold us if we continue like this!" she said, laughing and crying at the same time.

I took some tissues out of my pocket and wiped her cheeks before wiping mine; then I put a stray strand of her hair back in place. She moved over so I could sit down. I went past Declan, who was holding his father tightly around the waist, and sat down next to Edward, who took my hand in his, interlacing our fingers. The service began. I knew that Ireland was very religious, but their fervor surprised me; yet it didn't make me feel uncomfortable, even though I didn't believe in anything and had been brought up in the most absolute atheism. The two times I'd been to Mass were for my wedding and Colin and Clara's funeral—my in-laws were religious.

Everyone was singing. It was beautiful, almost joyful, and created an atmosphere of profound peace. Death was sad but it was not an end in itself. That had a reassuring effect on me; I could hear Abby's words again: "I'll take care of them." The only one who wasn't singing was Edward, but his hoarse voice echoed in my ears with every prayer. Every now and again, he stroked the back of my hand with his thumb. When it was time to take Communion, he let go of me to take his turn, following Jack and Judith. I sat back down and Declan climbed onto my lap, his hands tight around my neck. I rocked him. Edward came back and found us like that; he sat down and put his arm around my shoulders. We formed a single person; Declan crying, sitting on my lap, between his father and me, my head leaning against Edward's shoulder, his head resting on mine.

The moment I feared arrived: saying farewell to the departed. Everyone walked past. I clung more tightly to Edward, who held me even closer. When it was the family's turn—and since I was one of the family—he stood up, took Declan, and held him in his arms. Then he offered me his hand; I clenched it tight. Standing in front of Abby's coffin, he lovingly said goodbye to his aunt. Then he stepped aside so I could move forward, my hand in his, still holding his son. I placed my other hand on the wooden coffin and gently stroked it, a little smile on my face. The tears rushed down my face; I silently asked Abby to forgive me and entrusted Colin and Clara to her care. By this simple gesture—a gesture I'd refused to make for my beloved ones—I let them go, for I knew they were safe, especially my daughter. Thanks to Abby and the messages she had endlessly sent me, I finally accepted the idea that Clara would always be in my heart, that I had the right to a full, happy life, and that I would neither forget her nor betray her by living it. I no longer had to deny a part of myself. I felt Edward kissing my hair, and looked deep into his eyes. The intensity of the moment we shared was immeasurable. Declan was staring at us; I stroked his cheek. Then we went back to our seats. The service finished with "Amazing Grace," which moved me deeply. I wished I was a believer at that moment. Everyone gradually left. We were the last ones to come out into the fresh air. The weather was so nice; a luminous winter sky, the invigorating cold, a wind that carried away our unhappiness. Declan slipped his hand in mine; he wanted to whisper something to me.

"I don't want to stay here, Diane."

His terrified eyes stared at the graves.

"I'll see what I can do," I replied.

I didn't have to look for his father; he was right next to me.

"Declan wants to go now."

"He can't!"

"Please, let me take him away . . . "

He looked at his son with an expression that was both nervous and terribly worried. I decided to insist. Declan was still clutching my hand. He'd already suffered enough; the lioness in me took hold.

"He already knows how hard life can be for a child his age. Think about what he went through a few months ago; don't make him see another person he loves disappear into the ground . . . Please . . . I can take care of him; and you should take care of your little sister, she's the one who needs you," I added, seeing Judith looking so forlorn.

He knelt down to his son's level.

"You can go home with Diane, but first we have to see Jack together."

We went and kissed Jack, who thought it was a very good idea that I take Declan for a walk. His strength was incredible, and contagious. Who would have the indecency to break down before such dignity? Before leaving, I hugged Judith tight for a few moments, with Declan still holding my hand. Edward walked us to the gate of the cemetery.

"I'll come and find you later," he said, his voice sounding slightly panicky.

I stroked his cheek; he closed his eyes.

"See you very soon."

He turned around and put his arm around his sister and walked her to the graves. Their parents must also be there.

We quite naturally gravitated toward the beach, after letting out Postman Pat, who jumped all over his little master. I found a rock to sit on and lit a cigarette while they played. The ability children had to recover was breathtaking. Less than a quarter of an hour before, Declan had been terrified, traumatized, his eyes full of tears. All it had taken was his father's agreement, my hand, and his dog to comfort him. After he'd let off some steam, he came over and sat down next to me.

"Why does everyone die?"

Why? If only I knew, I thought.

"You're not alone, Declan, you have daddy, Jack, and Aunt Judith."

"Yes, but what about you? Are you still going away? I really like it when you're here."

"Me too, I like being with you, but I don't live in Mulranny."

"That's dumb!"

I sighed and held him in my arms. I could have answered Felix: I did love the "kid." Far too much.

"Aren't you cold?" asked Edward, when we heard him behind us.

He sat down next to his son and stared at the sea for a few seconds before looking at us. His eyes were slightly red.

"We're going to Jack and Abby's to warm up before you freeze. You're the only ones not there. You must be hungry, right?" he asked his son.

Declan took off like a shot, which made us laugh. Edward helped me up.

"Are you all right?" I asked, worried.

"Better since I found you two. Thank you for forcing me to spare Declan; I wanted both of you with me, it was selfish."

"No, it's normal. But you chose what was best for your son. And we're here now."

When we got there about ten minutes later, I could see everyone was waiting for us, given the number of people shouting "There they are!"

The hours that followed were full of conviviality, warmth, and comfort. Everyone was talking, patting each other's backs or holding hands, and recalling their memories of Abby in a loving atmosphere. Her generosity, her *joie de vivre* had touched everyone there. She had been a mother, a grandmother, a best friend, a nanny . . . Jack, through his kindness towards everyone, had been handed the torch, and didn't allow himself to be overwhelmed by his pain. He was proud, but I caught him looking into the distance several times, or instinctively stroking the plaid blanket that covered his wife's rocking chair. I remembered that feeling of loneliness when Colin and Clara died, even though I had flown into a rage and refused to accept reality; everyone comes to see you, tries to console you, but nothing works, you still feel empty. I was helping Judith in the kitchen; we were the two young women of the household. Declan ran between the guests, dashing here and there but regularly coming in to make sure I was still there. Edward and I continually tried to catch each other's eye; I sensed he was always close by and I was overcome by a need to make sure he was all right. At no time did I ever feel like a stranger in this community that was mourning the loss of one of its members. Quite the contrary, everyone naturally made me feel I was one of them, whether I wanted to be or not, regardless of my actual address. I was linked to the sadness of Jack, Judith, Edward, and Declan. To all these town people, I was part of the family. I could feel it in the way they looked at me, how they talked to me, how worried they were about me. A part of me was filled with happiness because of this recognition, this new feeling of belonging to a clan; but another part was drowning in sadness. I didn't, and would never, live among them. I'd rebuilt my life in Paris, where Olivier, Felix, and the bookstore were waiting for me. I would only have fleeting moments with this family, and no matter how wonderful they were, those moments didn't last. I looked at Edward, who was talking with a couple from the village. For a moment, I could barely breathe. Could I continue to repress my feelings for him for another two days? I needed to get some air; I discreetly went outside. While smoking a cigarette that I hoped would relax me, I forced myself to calm the pounding of my heart. It was dark, the cold air had become biting; I hugged myself to warm up. Deep inside, I wished for just one thing, and it happened.

"Are you all right?" asked Edward, who had come out to find me.

I shrugged my shoulders in reply. He lit a cigarette, held it between his lips as he took off his jacket; he put it around my shoulders. I looked up at him; he was staring out into space. We stayed there until we'd finished our cigarettes without saying another word. What good would it have done?

When we got back inside, I noticed that Declan was stretched out on the couch, fighting to keep his little eyes open.

"Look at your son, he's asleep on his feet . . . I could take him home. You stay with Jack and Judith a little longer."

"Are you sure?"

Without replying, I walked over to Declan and suggested we go home; he agreed immediately. I took his hand and went with him to say goodbye to Jack and Judith. He gave them each a big hug. Jack took me in his arms.

"Will you come and see me tomorrow?" he asked.

"Of course, I won't leave before spending some time with you."

"Oh . . . I won't keep you long; I'd rather you took advantage of being with them," he replied, nodding toward father and son.

I gave him a little smile before hugging Judith. Then I joined Edward, who was giving us a lift home before coming back. The owner of the pub and his wife stopped in front of us and offered us a ride in their car. Edward was about to refuse when I cut in.

"Thank you very much, that's very kind."

Then I turned to Edward, who looked more annoyed than ever.

"Don't worry, you'll be with us soon . . . "

He sighed and gave in, but insisted on walking us to the

car. Declan climbed in first, into the back, while Edward thanked our driver. He didn't drag it out, and came back over to me before I got in the car. I anticipated his reaction.

"We're not going to disappear, we're going back to your place and get into bed. Spend some time with Jack and Judith. Your son and I are fine."

He put his arm around my waist and pulled me toward him, kissing my forehead for a long time.

"See you back home," he whispered in my hair.

Those few words succeeded in echoing the feelings and desires I had buried deep in my soul.

Declan and I got home safe and sound. Postman Pat was barking his head off behind the door. The poor thing . . . I opened the door and he jumped all over us before heading off to the beach in the darkness of night. I took Declan upstairs where he put on his pajamas without saying a word and obediently brushed his teeth while I got his bed ready. He came back into his bedroom and slipped under the covers, still in silence, an anxious, inscrutable expression on his face.

"I'll stay with you."

I knelt down, stroked his hair, humming the lullaby, while he pressed his face against his mother's scarf. The day had been exhausting; he couldn't fight it. I put my head next to his on the pillow and looked at him. This child was so brave, he faced the challenges life threw him without complaining, or hardly ever! I so wanted to protect him and offer him the carefree life of a child. It was essential to do everything possible so he would be spared in future. When I was certain he was fast sleep, I silently left the room.

I went back downstairs and let Postman Pat back in, who had been patiently waiting outside the front door. I decided to go to bed, too, or at least to lie down, without going to sleep, in case Declan woke up. The dog followed me upstairs. But there was a surprise waiting for me in my bed: a little intruder who had found a way to drag himself into his father's room and climb into my bed, despite being half asleep. He opened his eyes and stared at me, looking sheepish.

"Can I sleep with you?"

I smiled sweetly at him.

"I'll be with you in five minutes."

He sighed with relief; I went into the bathroom and closed the door. Once ready, I sat down on the edge of the bathtub. I was doing far more than I thought I could; all my defenses were breaking down with this child. I no longer felt like some distant friend of the family and there was nothing I could do about it.

Postman Pat was sleeping at the foot of the bed; Declan was waiting for me under the warm blanket. I left the door open and the bedside lamp on, and got into bed. He snuggled up to me and I held him tightly in my arms, kissing his forehead. It didn't take him long to fall back into the arms of Morpheus. I breathed in his scent while thinking about Clara. I was certain she wouldn't be angry with me, that she knew that no one could ever replace her, she would always be my daughter, the greatest gift life had ever given me. But my heart was big enough to hold other children, there was plenty of space to fill, I loved children, I'd always loved them, and I'd dreamed of having a big family, because I was an only child.

Declan, like his father a year before, had dressed one of my wounds, perhaps the worst one, the most painful and deep-rooted. His distress and his personality had shaken me up, made me realize that I couldn't fight who I was: a dormant mother, but also a mother who was constantly evolving. The loss of Clara would remain engrained in my soul till my dying day, but I had learned how to live with that loss and would continue to learn as long as I lived. One person had known this before me: Felix. I could still hear him saying in his off-hand way: "One day, you'll come around again!" And stubbornly locked into my bleakest thoughts, I had assured him it would never happen.

Every now and again, I dozed off. The front door closed in the distance. Postman Pat raised his head and I gestured at him to stay. His tail was beating against the floor; his master was home. Edward stopped in front of the open door of his bedroom and found his son and me in his bed. He stood at the threshold for a long time, looking at us. Then he came over to us. He put his hands and one knee on the mattress.

"I'll take him back to his bed," he said quietly.

"No, leave him here, you'll wake him up and he's fine here."

"It's not where he belongs."

"Ordinarily, I'd agree with you! But today, he should be able to do what he wants."

I sat up straight. We looked at each other defiantly. I wasn't giving in.

"Daddy," Declan grumbled in his sleep.

We both looked at him; he opened his eyes slightly, pulled away from me and looked at us.

"You're going back to your room," Edward insisted. "Let Diane be; I'll stay with you."

Declan rolled into a new position, rubbing his face against the pillow.

"Let's all sleep together, Daddy . . . "

I wasn't expecting that, and neither was Edward! Declan grabbed his hand.

"Come on, Daddy," he murmured.

Edward looked deep into my eyes; I stretched out again and smiled at him. He let go of his son's hand and sat down on the edge of the bed, his back to me. He rested his elbows on his knees and held his head in his hands. I knew what he was thinking, I was thinking the same thing: we both wanted to protect and reassure this child, which meant we would have to suffer and put ourselves in an impossible situation. Untenable.

"Are you sure?" he whispered, without looking at me.

"Yes. Come to bed."

He stood up and walked around the bed to switch off the lamp. I could hear him moving around the room and taking off his clothes before getting in bed with us. The mattress sank and the covers moved. I turned over on my side to face him. My eyes got used to the darkness and I could see him: he was looking at me, one arm folded under his head. I fell asleep while watching him, without even realizing it. I felt good, at peace, with a little man in my arms and a grown man who made me forget everything that wasn't him.

10

Someone was tapping my arm. I slightly opened one eye: Declan was trying to wake me up. He succeeded. I felt something heavy on my stomach; Edward's arm nailed us both to the mattress, his son and me, while the bed's owner was in a deep sleep.

"We'll go and have breakfast," I whispered to Declan. "No noise, let daddy sleep."

I lifted Edward's arm from my waist as gently as I could. As soon as he was free, Declan leapt out of bed. Postman Pat, who hadn't budged all night, also got up and wagged his tail. I got out of bed, keeping the dog from getting closer and waking up his master. Declan and Postman Pat both went downstairs. Before closing the door, I glanced at Edward one last time; he'd moved over and was lying diagonally across the bed, his head on my pillow. How could I ever forget that sight?

Declan was waiting for me, sitting on a high stool at the counter. I put on one of his father's sweaters that was lying around and started getting breakfast. Ten minutes later, we were sitting side by side, Declan with his bread and jam and hot chocolate, and me with my coffee. I was instinctively slipping into family life, with no reservations and no fears.

"What are we doing today?" Declan asked.

"I'm going to see Jack."

"And after that? Are you staying here with us?"

"Of course, don't worry."

He seemed reassured for a while. As soon as he'd finished eating, he jumped down and put on the television. I filled my cup again, grabbed my pack of cigarettes and phone to sit on the porch, braving the cold. I felt bad when I saw the number of missed calls and texts from Olivier. I hadn't been in touch with him at all, hadn't thought about him for a single second. Trembling, I lit a ciggy before dialing. He picked up at the first ring.

"My God! Diane, I was so worried about you."

"I'm so sorry . . . yesterday was so awful . . . "

"I understand . . . but don't leave me without any word from you like that again . . . "

I briefly told him about the funeral and the evening that followed, omitting the emotions and confusion I'd experienced. Then I changed the subject to ask about Paris and the bookstore . . . Within seconds, I had the feeling he was telling me about a life that was not my own, one that had nothing to do with me. I stared at the raging sea as he explained that

Felix was proud of the takings for the past two days and that he'd gotten started on a new series of themed evenings. That hardly intrigued me or made me feel happy at all. I tersely replied things like "that's good." The bay window opened behind me, so I turned around, expecting to see Declan; I was wrong. Edward, his hair still wet from the shower, came out with his coffee and cigarettes and joined me. We look into each other's eyes.

"Olivier, I have to go."

"Wait!"

"What is it?"

"Are you coming home tomorrow? Are you really coming home?"

"Uh . . . why are you asking me that?"

"You're not staying there?"

I didn't stop staring at Edward; he couldn't understand what we were saying, but seeing the intensity in his eyes, I knew he realized it was important. Tears came to my eyes. My heart was going to break, no matter what I did. But I gave him the only possible answer.

"Nothing's changed; I'm coming back tomorrow."

Edward breathed in deeply and went to sit on the railing of the porch, a little away from me. Through the bay window, I could see Declan playing with his toy cars. The dog was watching him out of the corner of its eye. I felt Edward so close yet so far from me. I was going back to Paris the next day.

"That's good," I heard Olivier say in the distance.

"Don't come and get me at the airport, it's not necessary . . . Big hug."

"Me too."

"See you tomorrow."

I hung up. I smoked another cigarette, my back to the sea. Neither of us said a word. After putting out my cigarette, I decided to go back inside.

"I'm going to get dressed; I have to go and see Jack," I said to Edward, my hand on the doorknob.

I went upstairs without saying anything to Declan, grabbed some clean clothes from my suitcase, and locked myself in the bathroom.

The room was filled with the scent of Edward: the steam from his shower on the mirror, the smell of his soap. I stood under the shower for a long time, biting my fist, letting my tears flow. My desires, my feelings mattered so little: responsibility and logic were all that counted. I only had twenty-four hours left with them. Then, I was leaving.

When I came out of my hiding place, I heard Edward and Declan close by: they were in the office. I walked over and leaned against the doorframe. They were sitting in front of the computer where Edward was touching up some photos, asking his son what he thought of them. They really had become close, they were two of a kind. I had never gone into that room. It wasn't the usual chaos that caught my eye but a black and white photo pinned to the wall above the screen. It was very dog-eared and must have been handled many times to get into such a state . . . It was the entrance to Happy People, and you could just make me out behind the window; I was smiling, staring out into space. Everything about it made it look as if it had been taken in secret. When had he taken it?

The day he came to see me? That was impossible, I'd spent all day watching the street, I would have definitely noticed. So he'd come to be close to me, without trying to see me. The words he said several months ago echoed in my ears again: "There's been no room for you in my life for a long time now."

"Diane! There you are!"

Declan's voice made me jump and reminded me that now wasn't the time to ask for explanations.

"What are you doing?" I asked, walking into the room.

"I've got a bit of work," Edward replied.

"Declan, would you like to go with me to see Jack?"

"Yes!"

"Then off you go to get dressed!"

He raced out. I couldn't manage to leave the room and yet, I couldn't look at Edward.

"You'll be able to work in peace. Come and join us when you like."

I could sense him coming closer to me.

"What time is your flight tomorrow?"

"Two o'clock . . . Let's not talk about it, all right? Let's just enjoy today."

I looked up at him. We stared deeply into each other's eyes, our breath quickening, and I knew that I wanted more during our brief time left together. Our bodies gently touched.

"OK! I'm ready!"

I leapt back, putting some space between us.

"Let's go!" I said to Declan, rather loudly.

I walked out of the room, reeling a little. Declan said

goodbye to his father and we went downstairs to put on our coats, scarves, and hats; the weather was bad that day.

"Off we go!"

I whistled for Postman Pat, who trotted over. I opened the front door and Declan slipped his little hand in mine.

"See you later," I heard from behind me.

I looked over my shoulder; Edward was watching us from the top of the stairs. We smiled at each other.

The walk, that normally took twenty minutes, lasted almost an hour. I was constantly running after Declan, playing with him, laughing with him, as if I was trying every way possible to engrain him in my memory, not to forget him, to remember his strength, his instinct for survival, to cherish him. Or simply because I loved him and would soon be leaving him. That seemed utterly unbearable.

We raced each other into Abby and Jack's garden. Thinking about this house without thinking of Abby would remain unimaginable for a very long time. Jack was pulling out weeds from one of his wife's flowerbeds. I knew what he was trying to do: keep busy to forget by doing everything he could to be with her . . . The ambivalence of mourning.

"Well here you are, my little ones! What a welcome!"

Declan had jumped into his arms. Jack gestured for me to join them and hugged me tight.

"How are you this morning?" I asked. "Did you get some sleep?"

"Let's say I got up early!"

He put Declan down.

"Well . . . you can't get bored here! This isn't what I'd call a vacation!" said Judith.

She stood at the doorstep with her hands on her hips, wearing clothes for battling with the housework.

"Stop moaning, I'll come and help you!"

She was getting the house back in order after the dinner of the previous night. I rolled up my sleeves to give her a hand. It took us the rest of the morning to finish. The atmosphere was tranquil. Abby's absence weighed heavily, of course, but without being oppressive. Judith and I talked about her, laughing, but also sometimes shedding a tear.

Around noon, Jack came inside with Declan and lit a fire in the fireplace. I sent Judith to have a shower and got started on preparing the meal. I was watching the cooking when I looked out of the window and saw Edward parking his car. I didn't move. I soon could hear him talking to Jack, asking where I was. A few seconds later, I wasn't alone in the kitchen. He came up next to me.

"Do you need some help?"

"No," I replied, quickly glancing at him. "All that's left to do is set the table."

"I'll do that with Declan."

He called his son and in the end, all three of us set the table. Jack wanted to help. I stopped him, handing him his newspaper and forcing him to stay in his chair: "You're a guest in your own house today!"

I was happy to make him and Edward laugh. I was carrying in the big pot of food when Judith came in. She stopped for a moment when she found all three of us busy around the table. She stared straight at me, then looked at her brother before shaking her head.

Lunch lasted a long time; Declan finally couldn't sit still. He was between me and his father, squirming around in his chair. I leaned over to him.

"What's wrong?"

"I'm bored."

I smiled at him and nodded toward his father, who understood what we were plotting and winked at me.

"Take the dog and go outside," he suggested.

He rushed away. I called him back; it was stronger than me.

"Dress up warm, it's cold out."

"I promise!" he shouted from the front door.

"He's going to go out like a light tonight," I said to Edward.

"So much the better."

We smiled at each other.

"Dammit!" cried Judith, "You're going to screw up!"

My shoulders drooped. She was right.

"Let them be, please," Jack cut in.

"I'm saying it for both of you," she continued, "and for him."

"You don't have to remind us," her brother replied, coldly, "We know."

He clenched his fists on the table. I put my hand on his arm to calm him down; he looked at my hand for a moment before looking at my face. Then he took my hand in his and spoke to his sister.

"Can you look after him tomorrow morning and drop him off at school? We have to leave early for the airport."

"Of course!"

"Wait a minute!" I cut in. "This is ridiculous, Edward. I can manage by myself, hire a . . . "

"Don't even think it!" he said, stopping me, squeezing my hand even tighter.

"Now, now, children! Calm down," said Jack.

His intervention worked; the three of us looked at him.

"Diane and Edward, go outside and get some fresh air with Declan, then go straight home. Judith, go out and have a good time with your friends."

Brother and sister protested; I did nothing, just watched Jack. He didn't want to be a burden and needed to be alone, alone with the memory of his wife. He raised his hand to stop them talking.

"No point delaying getting on with your lives . . . I'm not afraid of being alone. I'll lead my quiet life; don't you worry about me. In any case, I wouldn't be staying with you this afternoon; I'm going to visit Abby."

No one tried to contradict him. He stood up and started clearing the table. I hurried to help him, and Judith and Edward did, too. In no time at all, the dining room was tidy and the dishwasher on. Edward hugged his uncle and went outside to join Declan in the garden. Judith came over to me.

"I'm so sorry about my outburst, but I'm worried about the two of you."

"I know."

"See you tomorrow morning," she said, then walked out of the kitchen.

Jack and I were alone. He gave me a big smile and opened his arms. I took refuge in them.

"Thank you for coming, my little Frenchwoman . . . "

"It was where I belonged. Take care of yourself . . . "

"You know this is your home."

"Yes," I whispered.

"I won't say any more. You know everything there is to know . . . "

I stroked his bushy white beard and ran out of the kitchen. Edward, Declan, and Postman Pat were in the car. I climbed into the Range Rover and slammed the door shut.

"Where are we going?"

I looked deep into Edward's eyes, questioningly. Behind me, I heard Declan's seat belt open; he came up between us, leaning on our head rests. I could feel all of Edward's questions, all his hesitations.

"We still have a few hours," I said to him.

His reply: start the car and drive off.

The rest of the afternoon flew by. Edward showed me another small part of the Atlantic Wild Way. He drove to the first cliffs of Achill Island. Declan monopolized the conversation by pretending to be a tourist guide. Edward and I looked at each other knowingly while listening to him show off his knowledge. We tempted the devil by getting out of the car while it was pouring with rain. And we went back home to the cottage soaked to the bone. Edward first lit a fire in the fireplace and sent his son to have a shower. I followed him upstairs and put on some dry clothes. While Declan was washing, I remade his bed, tidied up the mess in his room, and got his things ready for school the next day. When he came in, he walked over to me.

"Would you read me a story?"

"Choose some books and we'll go downstairs with daddy."

We sat down on the couch; I put my arm around him and he snuggled up to me. I started reading. I had a flashback of my aborted attempt at doing a reading session for children at Happy People. I realized how far I had come. One question still remained: if he had been a child I didn't know, would I have been able to do it? Not so sure. I loved Declan, and I wasn't afraid to admit it to myself any more. I wanted to keep the place he'd made for me in his life.

At certain moments, I looked up from the book and found Edward watching us. He'd also changed his clothes and was making dinner. The depression that had spread through me must have shown in my eyes, and in his, I could see his usual anger as well as sadness. I thought to myself that it had been a long time since I'd seen him show his feelings. We forced ourselves not to show our anxiety to spare Declan. And besides, did we really have a choice?

At the table, Declan was fighting to keep his eyes open, which had the effect of calming his father down; Edward looked at him affectionately.

"You're going to sleep in your own bed tonight," he told him.

"OK . . . "

He must have been really exhausted not to try and negotiate. Edward frowned.

"Judith is going to take you to school tomorrow."

"OK . . ."

"Do you want to go to bed now?"

He just nodded his head. He got down from his chair and took me by the hand. I got up and followed him, ready to go upstairs, but he made a detour toward his father and grabbed his hand as well. And I thought: be brave again. Edward and I looked at each other, then he lifted his son into his arms and Declan put his arms around his him, without letting go of me. Once in his room, Edward put him down on his bed and pulled the covers over him. I knelt down near his face. He automatically held his mother's scarf against his nose. With his free hand, he stroked my cheek. I closed my eyes.

"Don't go, Diane."

His words made me ache inside.

"Go to sleep, my little one. We'll see each other tomorrow."

He had already fallen into the arms of Morpheus. I kissed his forehead and stood up. Edward was waiting for me at the door, his face looking strained again. While walking down the hallway, the open door to his office attracted my attention; I went inside without asking his permission and took the photo off the wall.

"When did you take this?"

"What difference does it make?" he said, standing at the entrance to the room.

"Please . . . Tell me."

"The morning of the exhibition."

His voice was weary. My shoulders drooped and I felt a lump in my throat. The complexity and impossibility of our relationship, its difficulties, secrets, silences, the feelings we'd buried exhausted both of us.

"Why do you keep it?"

"As a reminder."

He turned away and rushed down the stairs. I sat down at his desk, staring at the photo I held in my hands, looking at myself standing opposite my bookstore, where I lived my life. Undeniably, I looked happy. At that time, there were no dark clouds hovering over me; I had everything I needed to be happy. At least, that was what I thought . . . For a few hours after it was taken, everything had been turned upside down, and ever since, I had totally lost control. The certainties about my choices, over which I had battled so hard these past few months, evaporated, one after the other. I ended up looking away from the image of this Parisian Diane, owner of a literary café, and Olivier's partner. I noticed a pile of photos that brought up other memories: the ones Abby had asked Edward to take when I'd come back the first time. We were all there in the picture, except for the photographer, but his presence was so strong that you could almost see him. As for me, I looked different, that much was certain. At no time did I seem to be distracted; I was there, looking straight at one of the others, or searching around for Edward. I had a place there and I had taken it.

Edward was sitting on the couch, smoking a cigarette, apparently absorbed by the fire in the fireplace, two glasses of whiskey on the coffee table in front of him. I did what I wanted to do, what I needed to do at that moment: I snuggled up against him, my head against his chest, my legs folded under me; he put his arms around me. We sat there in silence for a very long time; I could hear his heart beating and the wood crackling in the fire.

"Diane . . . "

I'd never heard him speak so softly, as if he were about to reveal some secret.

"I'm listening."

"Please don't ever come back here."

I leaned in closer to him; he hugged me more tightly.

"We can't delude ourselves," he continued. "Or pretend . . . "

"I know . . . "

"I refuse to make Declan pay for our past . . . he's too attached to you . . . he wants you to have a part in his life that you can't give him . . . He needs stability . . . "

"We have to protect him . . . we have no choice."

I rubbed my face against his shirt; he nuzzled my hair and kissed it.

"And I . . . I . . . "

He pulled away and quickly stood up, standing next to the fireplace, his back to me, his shoulders drooping. I also stood up and walked over to him. He looked over his shoulder and saw me.

"Don't . . . "

I stopped; everything hurt, my head, my heart, hurt to the very bone. Edward breathed in deeply.

"I don't want to suffer any more because I love you . . . it's unbearable . . . it's lasted far too long . . . That photo is no longer enough to remind me that you've built a life for yourself, a life in which you're not Declan's mother, not my wife . . . "

Did he realize what he was saying? His words and confession moved me deeply. He was truly telling me how he felt for the first time, and it was painful to both of us.

"Your life is in Paris, and will always be."

"That's true," I whispered.

He turned to face me and looked deep into my eyes.

"I have to forget you, once and for all . . . "

It sounded liked a promise and an insurmountable challenge.

"Forgive me," I said.

"It's no one's fault . . . we never had a future together . . . We never should have met, and we certainly never should have seen each other again . . . Get on with your life . . . "

"You regret having met me?"

He glared at me and shook his head.

"Go up to bed . . . it's better that way."

My first reaction was to do what he said; I turned around and headed for the stairs. Then I stopped. He didn't have the right to tell me all of that, to share his suffering without hearing about mine. What did he think? That it was going to be easy for me to draw a line under him and his son, to go back to Paris and pretend to love Olivier while I belonged to him body and soul, even if I was perfectly aware of the impossibility of our relationship? I turned to face him; he hadn't taken his eyes off of me. He pushed me away, to keep me at a distance.

"It can't end like this!"

"Diane . . . stop . . . "

"No, I won't stop! I have things I want to tell you!"

"I don't want to hear them."

The harshness in his voice made me move away, then I told myself that I'd had enough. I took his face in my hands and kissed him. He responded to my kiss passionately, locking his arms around me. I put all my frustration of the past months into that kiss. I stood on tip-toe, pressed myself against his body, trying to make myself smaller, to disappear inside him, to be even closer to him. I wanted more, more from him, more from his lips, from his touch. I had never felt such desire, never felt such a powerful urge to give myself to a man. Yes, he had been my crutch, but today, my feelings went far beyond that. At first, I hadn't loved him the way I should, but from now on, every fiber of my being, of my heart and body wanted him. I loved his strength and his weaknesses. With a painful moan, he tore himself away from me.

"We're going to hurt each other even more, stop, I'm begging you . . . "

"One night . . . we have one night left to pretend."

He was fighting so hard to control his emotions, he'd forbidden himself from living for such a long time, terrified by the pain of love and crushed by the responsibilities he took upon himself. I took his hand in mine and led him upstairs. I left him standing in front of his room while I made sure Declan's door was closed. He waited there for me, leaning against the doorframe. He stared deep into my eyes.

"There's still time to stop."

"Is that what you really want?"

He locked the door to his bedroom and pushed me toward the bed. If he had been weak and lost for a moment, that moment was over; I was powerless beside him. The harshness of his kiss made me sure of that. We fell onto the bed, in the grip of the urgency to make love, violently tearing our clothes off, finding each other's lips, touching our ravenous bodies. Declan was so close by that we had to be absolutely silent, and knowing we only had a few hours together added to the intensity of the moment we had waited for, and for so long: to belong to one another. When he entered me, I caught my breath and we looked deep into each other's eyes. In his, I read all the love and the desire he was feeling, but also all his suffering. I cried when Edward made me come. He collapsed on top of me; I kept him tightly between my legs and stroked his hair. Then, I took his face in my hands. He kissed me softly. The storm had passed.

"I love you," I whispered.

"Don't ever say that again . . . it changes nothing . . . "

"I know . . . but for a few hours, let's allow ourselves to do anything we want."

We made love all night, holding nothing back. Sometimes we dozed off, our damp bodies clinging to one another. And the first to open his eyes, awakened the other with kisses and caresses.

"Diane . . . "

I pressed my body even closer to his, clinging on to him even more, our legs entwined. He kissed me on the forehead.

"I'm going to get up . . . I don't want Declan to find us together."

His remark made me wake up completely.

"You're right."

I raised my head and stroked his tense jaw with one finger. He caught my hand and kissed my palm. Then he pulled away, sat down on the edge of the bed and ran his hands through his hair. He looked at me over his shoulder; I did my best to smile; he stroked my cheek.

"I'll go now . . . "

"All right."

I turned over, my back to him, for I didn't want to see him leave that room; I didn't want to remember that; all I wanted to remember was our night of love. I hugged his pillow with all my might as the door gently closed.

I stayed in bed for about half an hour. Getting up required superhuman effort, as well as picking up my clothes scattered all over the room. I fought against my old demons: I didn't want to wash so I would keep the scent of him on my body for as long as possible. But Edward wasn't dead.

Day had not completely dawned when I went downstairs. I put my suitcase in the front hall. A steaming hot cup of coffee was waiting for me on the kitchen counter; I drank it quickly. Then I went outside to the back porch, where Edward was smoking a cigarette. If he heard me coming, he didn't react. I pressed my body against his, took his hand in mine; our fingers locked. He sighed and kissed my hair. I closed my eyes, leaning against him. In the distance, we heard a car parking in front of the cottage.

"Here's Judith," he said.

I was about to pull away, convinced he would wish to keep our secret.

"No."

He let go of my hand so he could hold me tighter in his arms. I buried my face in his shirt, deeply breathing in his scent. The front door slammed: Judith and her legendary discretion.

"I'm going to have to go and wake Declan up," Edward said.

I clung on to his shirt.

"Let's go."

He led me inside. Judith was waiting for us, leaning against the kitchen counter, holding a cup of coffee. She smiled at us, somewhat sadly.

"Had to happen, since you've both been wanting it for so long . . . "

"Cut it out," Edward replied hotly.

"Oh, calm down! . . . I'm not criticizing you. I'm just jealous, that's all . . . "

We could hear Declan storming down the stairs.

"I slept all by myself! Daddy! Diane!" he announced, joyfully, "I slept all by myself!"

I had just enough time to move away from Edward before his son jumped into his arms. He was immensely proud; an amazing smile lit up his face.

"Did you see, Diane?"

"You're the best!"

His smile froze when he noticed Judith. His expression

reflected the violence of the reality that had just hit him. He freed himself from his father's grip and went into the front hall, head lowered.

"What's that?" he cried.

"My suitcase," I replied, walking over to him.

"What's it doing there?"

"I'm going home, remember?"

"No! This is your home now, with daddy and me! I don't want you to go!"

"I'm so sorry . . . "

Tears streamed down his face, he turned red with anger, rage, even.

"You're horrible!"

"Declan, that's enough!" Edward cut in.

"Leave him be," I whispered. "He's right . . . "

"I hate you!" Declan screamed.

He ran up the stairs and slammed the door to his room. Edward came over and held me in his arms.

"How could we have been so selfish?" I sobbed.

"I know . . . "

"Get going now," said Judith.

I pulled away from Edward and went over to her.

"I'm not going to say goodbye to you any more; I'm fed up with doing that. We'll speak on the phone . . . "

"You're right . . . "

Edward was waiting for me on the front steps, holding my suitcase. Just as I was about to go out, I stopped. It was all happening too quickly . . .

"I have to say goodbye to him."

I leapt up the stairs four at a time and knocked on his door.

"Go away!"

"Declan, I'm coming in."

"I never want to see you again!"

I went into his room; he was sitting on his bed, as stiff as a board. He furiously wiped his cheeks with the back of his hand, looking straight ahead. I sat down next to him.

"I'm so sorry . . . I made you hope I'd stay. You're right, I'm happy here with you and daddy, I like being here. I didn't lie about that . . . You'll understand when you're older . . . We can't always do what we want: I have a job in Paris, and the responsibilities of a grown-up. I know you couldn't care less about that . . . I'll think about you very often, that I can promise you."

He threw himself into my arms. I rocked him one last time, kissing his hair and holding back my tears. He wouldn't understand me leaving if he saw how sad I was.

"Come on, now . . . you'll be fine . . . you're a brave boy . . . I'll never forget you, never . . . You're going to grow up to be a big strong boy like your daddy . . . OK?"

I held him close for a long time; I wished I could always protect him, reassure him. But it was getting late . . .

"Daddy is waiting for me in the car . . . "

He hugged me even tighter.

"You'll see, you'll have fun going to school with Aunt Judith . . . and daddy will be back to pick you up after school. I got your uniform ready least night, so all you have to do is get dressed . . . "

He let go of me and looked at me with his beautiful eyes.

Then he sat up, put his arms around my neck and gave me a big kiss on the cheek, a real child's kiss, wet and sloppy. I kissed his forehead and he let me go. In spite of feeling I was abandoning him, I stood up and found that Judith had been watching us the whole time.

"Goodbye, Declan."

"Goodbye, Diane."

I walked across the room and stopped near Judith; we looked at each other and smiled, and I kissed her on the cheek before going downstairs. I found Postman Pat lying at the bottom of the stairs; I petted him one last time and went outside. Edward was leaning against the car, smoking a cigarette. I took one last look at the sea and climbed into the Range Rover. He got in after me and started the engine.

"Are you ready?"

"No . . . But I'll never be ready, so let's go."

I stared at the cottage for a few seconds through the car window. Then we drove off, passing through the sleepy village that was starting to come to life.

"Look who's there," Edward said.

In the distance, I could make out Jack, standing near his door. He raised his hand in our direction when we passed near him. I looked back over my shoulder; he stood still for a few seconds watching the car, then went inside, hunched over. When we left Mulranny, I grabbed Edward's cigarettes from the dashboard, took one, lit it, and dragged on it like a madwoman. I wanted to hit something, scream, release my anger. For the first time, I was angry at Abby: by dying, she had put me in an impossible position. I was perfectly aware of the egotistical, childish nature of my reaction, but it was the only way to fight my sadness. I was also angry with myself; I was nothing but a damned troublemaker! I made Olivier, Edward, Declan, and Judith all suffer. In the end, I was still as temperamental, awkward, and selfish as ever. You'd think that life had taught me nothing.

Merde! Fais chier! I swore in French.

While continuing to rant in even more colorful language, I grabbed my handbag, emptied it out on my knees and started going through it; I had to do something. When the burning ash from my cigarette fell on my jeans, I howled. Edward let me have my tantrum without complaining; he was driving as fast as he could, as usual. Little by little, I became less agitated. I calmed down, breathed more slowly; my throat was tense and my stomach in knots; I stopped fidgeting and sat back in my seat, relaxing against the headrest. Even though I was staring at the road, I didn't see the landscape.

After about an hour, Edward's phone rang. He answered; I didn't listen to the conversation, remaining stoical the whole time.

"That was Judith . . . Declan's better; he left for school in a better mood . . . "

That piece of news brought a little smile to my face, which quickly vanished. I felt Edward's thumb on my cheek, wiping away a tear. I turned and looked at him; he had never seemed so sad yet so strong. He was a father, and he felt all the pain his son felt. Even if it was something new to him, he made sure he came second: Declan was more important than anything. I felt the same . . . He stroked my cheek. He put his strong hand on my thigh, and I covered it with mine. Then he concentrated on driving again.

The drive went too quickly, much too quickly, with neither of us saying a single word. Edward continued wiping away my silent tears. I felt like someone condemned to die, waiting on death row. Life, and geography, were going to take away a man and a child I loved more than anything in the world. My only consolation would be knowing they existed, that they were all right. It wasn't the Grim Reaper who had taken them from me. It was "bad luck": we didn't live in the same country, didn't have the same life. We had given in to our feelings without taking reality into account.

When we arrived at the parking lot of Dublin Airport, Edward turned off the engine and neither of us made the slightest move to get out of the car. We sat there for about ten minutes. Then I turned toward him; he was sitting back in his seat, his head leaning backwards, eyes closed, his face tense. I stroked his chin; he looked at me with an intense expression. I saw the same love in his eyes as the night before, but with even greater sadness. He sat up, leaned over to me, and gently kissed me on the lips. That kiss grew more passionate. When he ended it, he took my face in both hands and leaned his forehead against mine. My tears wet his hands. He kissed me hard on the lips.

"We'd better go . . . "

"Yes . . . it's time . . . "

I could barely walk when I got out of the car. Edward threw my travel bag over his shoulder and took my hand. I held onto it with all my might, pressing my face against his arm. We went inside the terminal. My flight appeared to be on time. We were very early. That was also good; I wanted Edward to be back in time to pick Declan up from school; he shouldn't be apart from his father for too long. I preferred to check in right away to get rid of my suitcase. Edward never let go of me; the flight attendant looked at us closely.

"Are you traveling together?" she asked.

"If only that were possible . . . " he muttered softly, a stern look in his eyes.

"No," I said quietly. "I'm on my own."

Edward kissed my forehead again; I couldn't stop crying. The flight attendant glanced at us again and then looked down at the keyboard. In my mind, I thanked her for not wishing me a good trip. We walked away from the counter and I checked the time.

"You should go," I said to Edward. "I promised Declan you'd be there to pick him up from school . . . "

Pressed against each other, our fingers entwined, we crossed the departure hall until we got to security. I wanted to throw up, scream, cry. I was afraid of being without him again. But we had come to the point where Edward had to leave me. He held me close and hugged me tight.

"Don't drive like a maniac when you go back . . . "

He groaned painfully and kissed me on the forehead. I savored the feeling of that tender gesture, so full of meaning for him . . . Would I ever find the feeling of belonging to a man like this again?

"Don't say anything else," he said, his voice hoarser than ever.

I looked up at him; we shared a deep kiss, full of trembling pleasure and sadness. Our lips were seeking each other, tasting each other, memorizing each other. I clung onto his hair, his neck, stroked his chin; his hands wandered over my back, down my sides. The world around us no longer existed. But we had to separate. I pressed my body against him one last time, my face against his neck; he kissed my hair. Then I felt cold; his arms were no longer around me; he took a few steps back. We looked at each other one last time, promising each other everything, and nothing. I turned quickly around, my passport and ticket in my hand, and got into line. I instinctively looked back: Edward was still there, his hands in his jeans pockets, a stern look in his eyes, a serious expression on his face. Some of the passengers looked at him, afraid. I was the only one who knew he wasn't dangerous; he'd put his armor back up before their very eyes; he was protecting himself. I lost sight of him now and again through the line of travelers as I moved forward; each time it happened, I was afraid I wouldn't see him again, that it was the last time, the last second. But he didn't move. We were already about seven yards apart. I could feel him watching me when I had to empty my pockets, take off my belt, and remove my boots. I happily let the passengers in a hurry go ahead of me. The metal detector would mean it was over. But I had to steel myself to move forward. I stood on tiptoe and saw him once again; he already had a cigarette between his lips, ready to light it once outside. He took a few steps toward me, passing one hand over his face. I broke down and started crying. He saw, walked closer to me, shaking his head, asking me to stop, to be brave.

"Madam, you're next please."

Edward froze. In spite of the distance, we looked deep in each other's eyes.

"Yes, I know," I said to the security guard.

I went through the metal detector, crying, looking back behind me. Then Edward disappeared. I stood at the end of the conveyer belt in my socks for a long time, my bags getting crushed by the other suitcases piling up, before deciding to stagger to the departure gate. The other passengers looked at me as if I were from Mars. As if seeing someone crying at the airport was something new.

Two hours later, I'd fastened my seat belt. I took out my phone and sent Olivier a text: "On the plane, meet me at the bookstore tonight." There was nothing else I could to say to him, and that made me sad. I turned off my phone. A few minutes later, the plane took off.

11

At Roissy Airport, I decided to treat myself to a taxi; I had no desire to find myself getting jolted around on public transportation. In the car, I got a text from Judith: "Father and son together again." That made me feel better for a second.

I paid the fare and went upstairs to my apartment without even glancing at the bookstore or Felix. When I saw the partially packed boxes in my studio, I was ashamed about my hypocrisy towards Olivier. I'd led him to hope he could have a relationship and a life I didn't believe in. I threw down my travel bag and slammed the door.

I went into my café by the back door, noticed there were a few customers—whom I didn't greet—and went behind the counter.

"Hi Felix," was all I said.

I picked up the accounts book and checked the figures for

the preceding days. More to do something with my hands than because I was really interested . . .

"Hello, Felix, how are you? It wasn't too shitty being all alone? Would it kill you to be nice to me!" Felix moaned.

I shot him my meanest look. He opened his eyes wide.

"What stupid thing did you go and do?"

"Nothing! Leave me the hell alone!"

"You're not getting away with that!"

"Take the afternoon off," I countered, "you must be tired!"

"No, I'm not, but you're sick!"

"Please Felix," I hissed. "I can't allow myself to break down now."

I clung onto the counter, gritted my teeth, and tried to control my breathing.

"OK. I'll leave . . . good luck . . . "

"Tomorrow, Felix . . . I'll talk to you tomorrow . . . I promise."

"No problem! I know you! You calm down just as fast as you get worked up."

I had to wait until closing time for Olivier to come. His shoulders were drooping as he pushed open the door. I stayed behind the counter, as if to keep a safe distance. He sat down on a bar stool and leaned on the counter, staring at me. I couldn't say a word. He looked all around him, to the left, the right, above and below, as if he were trying to memorize the place. I should have remembered how perceptive he was; he'd understood everything.

"Olivier . . . I can't pretend any more . . . "

"I've only myself to blame . . . I wanted to believe in us; I hoped I'd be stronger . . . Ever since the exhibition, from the very first moment I saw you with him . . . I've refused to face up to reality. And yet, I always felt that he was the one you loved . . . "

"Forgive me . . . "

"I don't want to know what happened between you, or when. What makes me sad is that he doesn't make you happy . . . "

"It's our situation that makes me unhappy, it's not his fault."

"His son?"

"The distance."

He lowered his head.

"If I'd had a child, you wouldn't have given me a second look . . . "

He was right.

"I won't stop . . . that wouldn't do any good. I'll call the real estate agent tomorrow to break the lease . . .

"I'll do it . . . "

"No."

He stood up, walked to the front door, opened it, and turned around to look at me. Olivier had been so good for me, taken care of me, been so patient, and I was pushing him away.

"Take care of yourself," he said.

"You too," I whispered.

He closed the door behind him and I collapsed on the counter. I was alone again, but I'd been honest with myself and especially with Olivier. At long last. I went around the bookstore putting out the lights and slowly climbed the stairs to my studio. I didn't even glance at my suitcase or the boxes, I just stretched out on my bed in the dark and stared at the ceiling. In my mind, I relived the past three days, the night spent with Edward, leaving Declan . . . I was in so much pain. I missed them more than was humanly possible; I felt empty. My studio, which up until now had been my protective bubble, the place where I could take refuge since I first returned from Ireland, now brought me no peace. It was a bit as if I were in transit, staying at some stopping point, before taking a leap into the unknown. I was afraid; this was no longer my home. Everything familiar was shattered.

The next day, I woke up at dawn. I opened Happy People more than an hour early. While drinking my third coffee, I thought about Declan, who must be getting to school, and Edward, who was probably on the beach with his camera, or in his office. How were they? Had they slept? Had Edward managed to hold up? Was he suffering as much as me? Missing me as much as I missed him? And what about Jack? Had Judith gone back to Dublin? Greeting my customers, helping them, smiling at them in spite of everything changed nothing and didn't chase away those thoughts, the uncertainties rushing around my mind.

Felix was nowhere in sight; I spent a good part of the day alone, observing, feeling the bookstore, thinking about all of them. I did my work like a robot. When I talked to the customers, I felt as if I was hearing someone else's voice, someone else was answering their questions. I was detached from every move I made, every normal work routine. A distance—a real gulf—had calmly, insidiously, been created. At certain moments, I held onto the counter, as if I were trying to keep my feet on the ground. I wished I had the gift of a psychic so I could mentally make contact with them in Ireland, asking them to remind me of my responsibilities, so they could make me go back to them, entice me again, make me whole again, fill the gap left in me from not being with Edward and Declan. I kept looking at the pictures of Colin and Clara I'd hung up—I called out to them for help, too; I needed answers. And then I thought about Abby; I knew what she'd tell me. I forbid myself from thinking about the future, that future . . . that impossible future. And yet, it obsessed me, and it was in my hands.

Felix finally showed up at the end of the day. He actually had come at closing time, to get a free aperitif. The customers had all left. That wasn't such a bad thing; we needed to talk alone. He went behind the bar, poured himself a drink, and glanced over at me. He must have realized that I also needed a pick-me-up and poured a glass for me. Then he leaned against the door, made a silent toast, and watched me as he drank.

"Where did you sleep last night?"

"At my place."

He tilted his head to one side.

"Ah . . . and tonight?"

"Still at my place."

"The move?"

"I'm not moving any more."

I swallowed a large drink of wine to put on a good face. Then I grabbed my best way to escape—my cigarettes—and went outside to smoke. Felix, as addicted as me, didn't take long to follow. He leaned against the doorway and sniggered.

"Dammit! I never thought you'd do it . . . "

Suddenly weary, I leaned my head on his shoulder. I was exhausted by constantly interrogating myself, by the decision that demanded such enormous courage, a decision that made me question my whole life, and most especially worn out by missing Edward and Declan after only twenty-four hours without them.

"Here we are again, all alone," he continued. "He's a good guy; you could have been happy with him . . . "

"I know . . . "

"Well, I don't want to say it, but . . . you really look stupid now!"

I stood up straight and stepped right in front of him. He found something to laugh about! He'd better watch out; I was in a volatile mood.

"And may I ask why I look stupid?"

"You have two guys who love you, one of whom has got right under your skin, and you're all alone. You've lost everything because of this business and it makes no sense at all. What are you going to do now? Mope about in your café? Wait for a third guy to save you from the other two?"

Felix had no idea the reaction he had just provoked. To start with, I owed it to him not to shout; I was suddenly calm, at peace with myself. And then, by saying out loud what I'd been quietly thinking, he'd given me my answer. I wouldn't lose my family a second time.

"Thanks, Felix, for your advice . . . "

"But I didn't give you any!"

"But you did, I promise you . . . I have a favor to ask you . . . "

"I'm listening."

"Can you cover for me tomorrow morning?"

"Fine . . . " he said quietly, "OK."

"Thank you!"

When I came out of the real estate agency at noon the next day, I felt slightly dizzy; I'd completed the first stage, the next one would be that afternoon. And if there were no bad surprises, everything would be set in motion the next day. All I'd have to do was wait. I found a bench and collapsed onto it. I would see it through to the end, just as certainly as I'd left for Ireland the first time. I took out my phone and dialed his number. He wouldn't answer, of course; I could picture him seeing my name on his phone. I didn't give up and called back, again and again. He answered at my fifth try.

"Diane . . . "

His hoarse voice made me tremble from head to toe.

"You can't call me . . . "

"Edward . . . I won't keep you long; I just have something I want to tell you."

He sighed, and I could hear the sound of his lighter clicking open.

"I've just come from a realtor . . . I put the bookstore up for sale. If you and Declan still want me . . . "

I was overwhelmed by my emotions. Edward said nothing. I started to get worried.

"Are you there?"

"Yes . . . but . . . that city . . . it's your husband and your daughter . . . you . . . "

"No . . . it's not them. I carry them within me. And now, there's you and Declan. What's happening to us is so rare . . . I refuse to spend my life without you two; you wouldn't be uprooting Declan . . . Neither of you would be happy living in Paris, but I would be happy living in Mulranny . . . "

"Diane . . . I can't let myself believe that . . . "

"But you can believe it. You and me, and Declan too, it's no longer a dream. I'll never be your son's mother, but I will be the woman who supports his father in raising him, and I'll give him all the love I can . . . And I'll be your wife . . . That could be our life, if you still want it . . . "

Several long seconds passed. Then I heard him take a deep breath.

"How could you even doubt it?"

Half an hour later, I walked through the door to Happy People, making its little bell ring. Felix was gabbing with some of the customers. His world was about to collapse. I went over to him, gave him a peck on the cheek, and poured myself a coffee.

"We need to talk," I said, without mincing my words.

"If I weren't gay, I'd think she was going to break up with me . . . "

Everyone burst out laughing, except me. He wasn't far off the truth.

"We'll leave you two alone!" the customers said, still laughing hysterically.

"OK, what's happening?" he asked when we were alone.

I looked straight at him.

"Two realtors are coming here this afternoon . . . "

"Yeah, so what?"

"They're coming to do a valuation on the bookstore."

He shook his head, opened his eyes wide, and banged his fist on the counter.

"You're selling?"

"Yes."

"I won't let you!" he shouted.

"What?"

"Why are you doing this?"

"I lost my family; I couldn't do a thing about it; it took time to accept that Colin and Clara would never come back. I'm not going to lose my family a second time. Edward and Declan are alive, they're my family, I feel at home in Mulranny, with Jack and Judith too . . . "

"And what about me?"

He was hysterical.

"What about me?" he continued. "I thought *I* was your family!"

I saw a few tears roll down his cheeks; mine were streaming down my face.

"You are and always will be my family, Felix . . . But I love Edward and I can't live without him . . . Come and live in Ireland with me!"

"Are you an idiot or something? You think I'd want to be the third wheel or the babysitter!"

"No, of course not," I replied looking down.

He walked away, picked up his coat, and lit a cigarette inside. I followed him, panicking.

"What are you doing Felix?"

"I'm out of here! I don't want to be here when . . . And I have to find a job; I'm going to have to collect unemployment because of you."

He'd already opened the door.

"No, Felix, you won't lose your job. I've asked the buyer to keep you."

"Yes, like the furniture!"

He slammed the door; it shook so hard I thought the window might shatter, then he ran down the street. The sound of the little bell echoed for a long time. For the first time, I had a feeling of impending doom. The violence of his reaction froze me to the spot.

But I didn't have time to dwell on Felix and his sadness, and even less on my own. The vultures from the real estate agencies showed up, one after the other. I watched them coldly dissect my café, answering their questions coolly and impartially. From now on, it was impossible for me to feel any emotion towards the bookstore, which soon would no longer be *my* bookstore. I had to get used to it, for the next day I would go and sign the seller's documents. No sign of Felix all day. I flooded his phone with texts and messages but nothing worked: not my apologies, not my threats to never see him again, not my sobbing. Once again, I had the impression I was becoming an adult, growing up. Every decision implied losses, leaving little pieces of my life behind. Nothing in the world would make me want to do without Felix's friendship; he was the brother I never had, my partner, my confidant, and my twin; my savior in my darkest hours . . . but I loved Edward more. In the same way, I would have given up Felix for Colin; and he knew that deep down. I hoped he would come to understand. Calling Edward at ten o'clock that night saved me from falling into a deep depression. While talking to him, I slipped into bed, wrapped myself in my blanket, and imagined up our future together. He was less expressive than me—I knew him—and I could tell he was still holding back, finding it difficult to let himself go. My decision was still abstract to him, hundreds of miles from Paris. He explained that he'd rather wait before talking to Declan about it—I understood. And of course, we were both conscious of the fact that it could take some time before I got that one-way flight.

At the end of the afternoon the next day, when there was a "For Sale" sign in the shop window, I decided to send Edward something concrete. I went out into the street, stood on the sidewalk opposite, exactly where he must have been standing to take the photo he'd hung up on his wall. It took a few seconds for me to stop shaking and get my breathing back to normal. How could I erase this sight from my memory: HAPPY PEOPLE READ AND DRINK COFFEE: FOR SALE. This, too, was part of my family, and I was leaving it all behind. I took the photo with my phone and sent it to Edward, along with a short text: "It's not a dream any more; it's no longer home." He immediately replied: "How are you?" How could I reply to that without worrying him? "Fine, but I miss the two of you." Then I got a photo that made me smile; Edward looked cheerful; he sent me a selfie of himself and Declan on the beach, smiling. I was just about to cross the street when I saw Felix, frozen in front of the sign in the window. I went over to him and put my hand on his arm. He was shaking.

"I'm so sorry," I said.

"Are you sure it's worth it?"

"Yes."

"How can you know?"

"Because of this."

I handed him my phone with the picture of Declan and Edward that took up the whole screen. He stared at it for a long time, still shaking. Then he sighed and looked at me, before staring out into space.

"I really should have smashed his face in, even if I went to jail . . . "

I gave him a little smile; he hadn't completely lost his sense of humor.

"Shall we go inside?"

I didn't wait for his reply; I took him by the arm and pulled him into the bookstore. I poured us each a glass of wine. He sat down next to the customers.

"Will you come back to see us?"

"I don't know . . . give me some time to get settled . . . "

A few days later, while I was opening up, I was overcome with emotion when I saw Olivier stop in front of the bookstore. I hadn't seen him since we broke up, which already felt like ages ago to me. Difficult to imagine that today was the day we were supposed to move in together. He pushed open the door and I noticed he was carrying a bag. He put it down near the stockroom, then came back and sat down at the counter.

"Could I please have your Happy People special blend of coffee? I could use it."

Two minutes later, I'd served him his coffee, then he broke the silence.

"It didn't take you long to decide," he sighed.

"I know . . . Olivier, please forgive me for hurting you . . . "

He raised his hand and I stopped talking.

"We were headed straight for disaster, especially me."

He drank his coffee in one gulp, stood up and pointed to the bag.

"I think I found all your things . . . "

"Thanks," I whispered.

He took a few steps towards the door then turned to look at me again. I stood stoically behind the counter. He gave me a little smile.

"I'll say goodbye, then. I won't be coming back; I found another route that avoids passing by here."

"I'm really so, so sorry."

"Stop apologizing. I don't regret having met you, or what we had together. I would have preferred a different ending . . . but . . . that's life . . . "

One last look and he was gone. Olivier was out of my life. Had I ever really loved him? I felt affection, tenderness towards him, but love . . . If I hadn't seen Edward again, perhaps my feelings for him would have grown. Or, more simply, I wouldn't have tried to sort reality out from what I was feeling. I'd never know, but what was certain was that the memories I had of him were now vague: all I could clearly see were the moments spent with Edward, the time with him and my Irish family. When I thought about them, my heart beat faster, I was finally at peace, full of a sense of completeness.

The month that followed was exhausting and nerve-wracking. Viewings increased . . . but never ended in a sale. Not one offer. I was getting depressed and impatient, while the realtors were kicking up a fuss because of Felix. They blamed him for the situation. In truth, he didn't make an effort. Yet he had assured me that he wanted to continue working at Happy People after I left. Every time a potential buyer stood in the doorway, he became unbearable, not serving the customers properly and barely replying to questions to get rid of him. The only time he spoke honestly was when he described his addiction to partying and sleeping late. I was incapable of putting him in his place; I'd never behaved like his boss and always considered him my partner. Out of the question to start now, just when I was about to abandon him. I'd hurt him enough. On the other hand, the realtors got a taste of my bad side when they asked me to remove Felix from the contract of sale. This was still my place and I intended to remain in charge right till the end. There wouldn't be any Happy People without Felix; that was a way of keeping a foothold there, a way not to completely turn my back on it and, above all else, I wanted to keep Felix.

That day, I was told there would be one more viewing, and it was my last chance. A few minutes beforehand, I took Felix aside.

"Please, don't make a scene . . . stop putting off the inevitable . . . "

"I know, I'm nothing but a little brat . . . "

He put his arms around me and held me close. He'd come back, at last. A little bit, at least. The little bell rang; Felix gave me a dark look and let go of me.

"I'm going out for a smoke."

He passed the realtor and his client, mumbling a vague hello. This wasn't over yet! I put on my brightest shopkeeper's smile and walked over to my guests. The realtor opened his eyes wide because of Felix; I ignored him and stretched out my hand to the man waiting beside him; he was looking around the place.

"Hello, monsieur, delighted to welcome you to Happy People."

He had an iron-like grip and looked me straight in the eye from behind his Clubmaster sunglasses. He was too serious, too impeccable for the bookstore, with his tailor-made suit and respectable, upper-class appearance.

"Frederic, pleased to meet you. It's Diane, isn't it?"

"Yes . . . "

"Would you allow me to look around at my leisure and we can talk afterwards?"

"Make yourself at home."

"I'm still only a guest, so I need your permission."

He walked around Happy People for nearly half an hour, ignoring the realtor who was hovering over him. He carefully examined every nook and cranny, leafed through some of the books, felt the wood on the counter, looked at the street through the window. He was still standing there when Felix decided to come back inside. They looked at each other, and my best friend took his place behind the bar. Frederic joined him, sitting down at the counter.

"Are you the person I'll be working with?"

"So it seems," my best friend said. "But I'm not in the mood to be interrogated."

So here we were again!

"I have everything I need," Frederic replied, still smiling.

He didn't seem shocked by Felix's attitude; he stood up and gestured for the realtor to follow him outside. They spoke for a long time on the sidewalk.

"I couldn't help myself, Diane . . . "

"It could have been worse; you made an effort. You avoided telling him that you sniffed coke from the counter, like you did with the last one."

"Did I really do that?"

Frederic opened the door and spoke to me.

"I know it's not a very conventional way of doing things, but I'd like to have dinner with you tonight to discuss Happy People and get some information I need. Would this evening work? Shall I come and pick you up?"

"Uh . . . "

"Eight o'clock."

He glanced over at Felix and left.

"Who is that guy?" Felix snickered. "Your Irishman wouldn't be happy, not in the least."

He burst out laughing.

"You're not wrong. But at least he made you laugh."

I described the stormy conversation with Edward by sending him a simple text: "Having dinner with a buyer; I'll call you after." I turned off my phone. At one minute past eight, the mysterious Frederic arrived, haughtily ignored Felix, and led me outside. We walked in silence to a restaurant on the Place du Marché-Sainte-Catherine, where he'd reserved a table. In spite of his odd attitude, I quickly felt very much at ease with him. He briefly told me about himself. He was a former managing director from La Défense who had a good amount of savings as he had no family to support. He wanted a change, but without leaving Paris, which was the only place he felt he could breathe freely. Then he wanted to know how Happy People had come about. The floodgate opened: I told him my whole life's story, Colin and Clara, my impossible period of mourning, the exile in Ireland, Edward, what he was like, his love, my love for him and his newly found son, and my decision to leave everything behind to start all over again with them.

"And Felix?" he suddenly cut in.

I launched into another chapter of my life and he was even more interested. I concluded by explaining to him how much selling the bookstore and my leaving hurt Felix, without hiding the truth from him.

"If you buy, things might be very difficult with him at first, but please, be patient, he's wonderful, and he's part of Happy People, he's more the soul of the place than I am."

"Diane, you're the most important woman in the world to him," he said, looking straight at me.

"Oh, let me stop you there; you're wrong, Felix is gay."

"I know . . . but all the same, I still maintain you're the one he loves, and he's losing you. He will have had you and his mother. I know what that's like."

He gave me a wry smile to confirm what I'd already understood.

"You always end up letting go of the gay man in your life for the love of your life. And he's never prepared for it."

He raised his hand to ask for the check and paid it without my being able to string two words together.

"I'll walk you back," he suggested.

I nodded, and we headed back to Happy People.

"I promise you I'll look after him," he said, breaking the silence. "He'll get over it, and come back to you, one day . . . "

"Wait a minute, Frederic! What exactly are you saying?"

"I'm going to buy your Happy People, and I'm counting on being very happy there myself . . . with Felix."

"Just a minute! You're going to buy Happy People?"

"That's what I said! You'll soon be back with your Edward and his son."

"But what about Felix? What do you plan to do with Felix?"

"Seduce him . . . "

My eyes opened as wide as they could.

"I don't doubt your ability to seduce anyone. But Felix has no concept whatsoever of monogamy."

"We'll see . . . "

I saw the look on his face and understood he'd succeed.

"I'll sort out everything with the realtors and come back to see you tomorrow. Have a good evening, Diane. Send my regards to Edward."

I started climbing the stairs of my building but stopped to pinch myself. The pain reassured me that tonight had really happened. When I got inside, I stretched out on the bed with my phone. As soon as he picked up, Edward barked.

"I absolutely forbid you to do that again! Who is this guy you spent the evening with?"

"The man who's in love with Felix and the new owner of Happy People."

"What?"

"You heard right . . . I'll be coming soon . . . very soon . . . and I don't have to worry about Felix any more . . . "

Everything happened quickly after that night. Since Felix had power of attorney for the bookstore, I didn't need to wait for the sale to be finalized, and I didn't want to. Frederic suggested he take my place to get used to Happy People and the work, hoping to bring Felix out of his shell as well. Felix made a scene, at first, then ended up accepting the situation, feigning indifference. For the moment, he saw nothing of his future boss's ploy. The day when it was right before his eyes, he'd find it really bizarre! Frederic was making himself indispensable. As for me, I let them size each other up and get their bearings while I prepared my big departure, the real one, the final one. I packed up all my things that would be transported to Mulranny in a few weeks; I closed my bank accounts and filled in hundreds of official documents. I spoke to

Edward and Declan on the phone every day. Or rather, to Declan! For Edward, who was already not very talkative, the telephone was a form of torture . . .

My last day in Paris. My flight was the next day. I'd spend my last afternoon at Happy People. In the meantime, I took the same route I'd taken every Monday for more than a year. I got out of the metro; my legs were shaking. I went into the closest florist, who knew me since I'd run away from her that first day. For the last time, I bought an armful of white roses from her and opened an account: every week, she was to place the same flowers on their grave. I gave her a friendly hug and headed for the cemetery. I took a long time to walk down the main path. Once in front of them, I got down on my knees and changed the flowers, throwing the wilted ones behind me. Then I stroked the marble gravestone.

"Oh . . . my loves . . . you will always be my loves. I'm leaving tomorrow; it's done . . . Colin, we already talked about it . . . You know I'll never forget you. I haven't replaced you with Edward . . . I love him, that's all . . . and you, my Clara . . . you might have had a brother like Declan . . . I'm not his mother, I'm still yours. My new life is starting tomorrow in a place you don't know, but which is now my home. I don't know when I'll come back to see you . . . but you'll both always be with me . . . If you can't find the way, ask Abby; she'll guide you to the beach . . . I love you both . . . I'll always love you . . . "

I kissed their tombstone one last time, a long, hard kiss, then I left, without looking back.

The afternoon sped by—customers came in one after the

other. I barely had time to turn around and suddenly it was nearly seven o'clock; my last day as the owner of Happy People was coming to an end. Being busy had helped me to not think about it.

"Dammit! I'm going to slam the door in the face of the next person who walks in!" Felix shouted.

Frederic came in at that very moment.

"Perhaps not, actually," he joked.

Frederic came over to me and kissed me on the cheek. He shook Felix's hand over the counter.

"I came by to wish you bon voyage."

"Thanks, that's kind."

We had very quickly gotten past speaking to each other formally. Fortunately, since I suspected that very soon he would be joining the ranks of my weird family . . . In any case, that's what I hoped.

"Come on, let's have a drink!" Felix suggested.

He got some champagne out of the fridge, popped the cork, and handed me the bottle, looking straight at me.

"Does this remind you of anything?"

"I'll never forget that evening, never!" I replied, my eyes full of tears.

"Don't worry . . . tonight we'll go easy . . . I don't think Edward would appreciate seeing you get off the plane tipsy."

I took a big swig straight from the bottle, then handed it to him. Felix nodded toward Frederic, who gestured no. Felix went over to him.

"You want to be one of the family? Then drink and prove it."

They looked at each other defiantly; for a few seconds, I felt like I was the third wheel. Their relationship was going to be volatile . . . Frederic drank and handed the bottle to Felix who went back behind the bar. The three of us knocked it back in two rounds.

"I'll leave you two alone. See you tomorrow," he said to Felix.

I walked him out.

"I'm entrusting them to you, both Felix and the bookstore," was all I said.

"They'll be in good hands."

"I have faith in you."

"See you soon, Diane . . . "

Felix was waiting for me, sitting on the counter, holding a new bottle. I climbed up and sat next to him, leaning my head on his shoulder.

"I can't talk to you, Diane. It's too hard . . . "

"Don't worry, it's OK."

"On the other hand, I'm going to buy you drinks and put it on my new boss's tab."

We spent the evening sitting side-by-side, emptying bottles, sometimes holding hands, smoking one cigarette after the other. Every now and then, Felix crushed me against him. And then he finally opened his mouth and asked me something that really shocked me.

"Don't take the photos on the board; leave them for me."

"They've always been yours. Are you going to put them in your apartment?"

"No, they'll stay here. I got the owner to agree: I explained that without Colin, Clara, and you, there would be no Happy People . . . "

An hour and a bottle later, I was showing signs of fatigue.

"Go to bed," he said. "You have a big day ahead of you tomorrow; you're going to be with your two men again. But first, there's one last thing I have to do."

He took a barstool and carried it next to the door. He climbed up on it and took down the little bell.

"You can't leave without something to remember us by . . . "

I broke down and threw myself in his arms, letting all the tears flow I'd been holding back the past few days. Felix held me in his arms.

"I can't face taking you to the airport tomorrow."

"It doesn't matter, because I don't want you to come."

We were whispering.

"What time is your taxi?"

"Seven in the morning."

"Leave the keys in the studio. Lock up one last time."

He stood up, took me by the shoulders and looked straight into my eyes.

"Bye, Diane!"

"Felix . . . "

He let go of me and walked out into the night. One last look through the shop window and he was gone . . . I wiped my cheeks with the back of my hand before taking the set of keys from my pocket. First job: lock the door. Second: turn the sign over. Third: put the notice in the window "Under new management." Fourth and final: turn off the lights. The bright streetlamps allowed me to see my café as if it were daytime. I'd chosen everything here with Colin, it was a part of me, even if I'd neglected it for a while—for too long—and I'd grown up in this place. When I came back—if I came back—I'd no longer recognize the place; it would have to change. The new owner had a very strong personality; he'd want to make his mark . . . That was normal; I wouldn't have a say in it. I strolled around the shelves, overflowing with books: well organized and ready to be bought. Then I went behind my counter and stroked the wood: sparkling clean. I put back a few glasses that were out of place. I straightened out the pile of accounting books and orders and the board with the photos. Then I stopped in front of the coffee machine, and smiled to myself, remembering the day I'd given Felix hell for not being able to clean it properly. I wanted to make myself a coffee but didn't; I knew I wouldn't enjoy it; it would taste reheated. I preferred not to remember my last one; that would remain a vague moment, suspended in time, with the background noise of the customers, Felix's laughter, the sounds from the street. It was time. I went through the back to the staircase. At the doorway, I stopped, closed my eyes and breathed in deeply—the smell of the books, coffee, and wood. Flashbacks, bits of memories rushed through my mind. I closed the door without opening my eyes, concentrating on the creaking hinges. Despite all my efforts, they had never stopped creaking. The click of the lock made me start: it was over. Happy People Read and Drink Coffee was going to live on without me . . .

Epilogue

I'd been living in Mulranny for over three months. I felt more and more at home with every passing day. My life seemed easy now, natural, I asked myself more questions and took the time to fully live, without regrets. I thought about Happy People every day, and it would be a lie to say that I never felt a pang in my heart, but it always passed very quickly. The idea of opening a bookstore was brewing in my mind . . . But there was no hurry.

I was on the phone with Felix. Impossible to get a word in! He kept thinking about the actions and behavior of Frederic, who kept him stewing for days and days. My best friend was smitten, and it was really the first time it had happened to him; he was the very picture of a teenager going through his first love.

"I can't take it anymore, I swear . . . last night, I was sure he was finally going to make a move . . . then nothing, he left me standing outside my front door!"

"So why don't you make the first move?"

"Huh, I don't dare . . . "

I raised my eyes to the heavens, stifling my mad laughter.

"Don't you go and make fun of me!"

"I'm sorry, I couldn't help myself . . . "

The front door closed behind me and I looked over my shoulder; Edward had come home from his assignment, soaking wet from head to toe. He dropped his equipment heavily to the ground and threw off his coat, grumbling. Then he noticed me and walked over, his face still looking tense. When he got to the couch, he leaned down and kissed me on the forehead, sighing. "Felix?" he whispered in my ear. I nodded. He gave me a little smile.

"Hey, Diane! Did we get cut off or something?" Felix shouted into the phone.

"Sorry, Edward just got home . . . "

"OK . . . Got it . . . I'll call you back tomorrow."

He hung up right away and I dropped my phone next to me. Edward still hadn't moved, one arm on each side of me, leaning against the back of the couch.

"I'm really starting to think I scare him . . . He cuts your conversations short as soon as he knows I'm here."

"No . . . he just doesn't want to bother us . . . And besides, I speak to him on the phone almost every day, so . . . "

Edward stopped me talking with a kiss.

"Hello," he said, after he'd stopped kissing me.

"I didn't hear you leave this morning . . . how was your day? Did it go well?"

"Perfect. The weather was just what I needed for what I wanted to do."

"Is that why you're in a bad mood?"

"More than usual?"

"No," I replied, laughing.

He kissed me again before standing up straight. Then I got up, too. He put on a dry sweater before helping himself to a coffee.

"I'm leaving in five minutes to pick up Declan," I said.

"Do you want me to go?"

"No, I have to stop by to see Jack afterwards, and I have some shopping to do."

He came over to me, stroked my cheek and frowned.

"Are you tired?" he asked.

"No . . . how could I be?"

"If you say so," he replied, not at all convinced.

He took his soaking wet pack of cigarettes from his pocket and went outside to the porch. I slipped on my coat to join him. I clung on to him. Edward regularly had moments of panic when he feared I'd regretted my decision.

"Don't worry . . . I'm fine; I've never felt so good."

I looked up at him; he was watching me, a harsh look on his face, as ever. I stroked his chin, let my fingers play through his beard; he grabbed me by the waist, pulled me against him and kissed me passionately. His way of saying that he was afraid of losing me. I couldn't understand how he might still fear that . . . I replied to his kiss with all the intensity of my love. I moved away from him, smiled, stole the cigarette he had in his hand, and took a few puffs before putting it back between his lips.

"See you soon!" I sang as I walked away.

He groaned. I walked through the kitchen, grabbed a package from the fridge, and picked up the car keys.

A few minutes later, I double-parked in front of the school, just in time: the children were coming out of class. I could see Declan's messy hair in the middle of the other children. He pushed his friends aside and ran towards me. He was afraid of the same thing as his father: that I'd suddenly disappear.

"OK, champ?"

"Yes."

"Come on, hop in!"

When we got to Jack's, we found him sitting in Abby's rocking chair, his newspaper folded on his lap, staring at the fire in the fireplace. He aged a little more each day; the cause of his lack of energy was becoming more and more apparent. The winter and the Christmas holidays had aged him by ten years. I was the only one he talked to about how unhappy he was; he knew I'd understand. I loved the time we regularly spent together, just the two of us. I went to see him at his house several times a week. Even though he complained, he let me put the place in order and prepare him some meals in advance. I wanted to force him to fight. I knew such a thing was selfish, but I wanted to spare Declan, Edward, and Judith, at least for a while. We all needed him. My greatest ally was this little boy who jumped all around the living room, asking him when they could go fishing again together.

"On Sunday, if you like," he replied.

"Really?"

"Yes! Diane and your father have some things to do," he said, winking at me.

I gave him a kiss on his chin and went into the kitchen to organize the food I'd made that morning.

"Do you need anything?" I asked, once I was sitting next to him. "We're going to do some shopping. And I need to stop in at the pharmacy, so tell me."

"No, I have everything I need. But don't dawdle. The weather's bad tonight."

"You're right! Declan, are you ready? Let's go."

The next morning, my eyes started to flutter open when I felt a kiss on my lips. Edward was leaning over me, smiling; he was looking at my face, his hands wandering over my body.

"What do you want to do this weekend?" he asked in his hoarse, sleepy voice.

"Sleep . . . "

"Stay in bed, then. I'm getting up."

"No."

I clung onto him, forced him to lie down again, and pressed my body against his, rubbing my nose against his bare chest. He didn't try to fight me, just held me tight as I sighed with satisfaction. I started kissing him all over, gradually climbing on top of him, and his hands over my body became more eager . . . Then we heard Declan's footsteps in the hall and the dog's yapping.

"I'll go," Edward grumbled, "I'll see if I can get Jack to let Declan sleep there tonight."

"Good idea . . . "

He got out of bed, picked his jeans off the floor and pulled them on, then went out into the hall, making sure that no intruder got into our room. I spread out on his side of the bed and dozed for nearly an hour.

When I finally decided to get up, I took longer than usual in the bathroom. Before coming out, I looked at myself in the mirror, stifling my laughter, tears in my eyes. I went downstairs, shaking slightly. Declan was stretched out on the floor, playing with his car set. When he saw me, he leapt up and jumped on me. I gave him a big hug, like I did every morning.

"Diane, I'm going to sleep at Jack's tonight!"

Edward hadn't wasted any time.

"Are you glad?"

"Oh, yes!"

He went back to his game, without taking any more notice of me. I poured myself a coffee at the kitchen counter and looked lovingly around. Declan was playing, relaxed, serene, like any little boy of his age. Postman Pat was snoring, his paws in the air in front of the fire in the fireplace. From the bay window, I could see Edward on the front steps, watching the sea, smoking a cigarette, pensive and at peace. My heart swelled with happiness. I'd come so far, we all had. We'd succeeded in creating a happy family out of broken, shattered people, and all was well . . . I took my coffee and went over to the man for whom my heart skipped a beat and with whom I shared everything from now on—everything and even more. Our eyes met and I gave him a smile that could move heaven and earth.

"Are you OK?" he asked.

"Yes, great, actually . . . "

Like every morning, he threw me his pack of cigarettes. I stared at it for a long time. Then I opened it, got a fix from the smell of the tobacco, closed my eyes, and threw it back to him.

"Are you sick?"

"Absolutely not . . . "

"Don't you want a ciggy?"

"Of course; I'm dying for one."

"Well then, what's wrong?"

Still smiling, I moved closer to him and snuggled up in his arms.

"I have to stop smoking, Edward . . . "

Thanks

To Roxana and Florian, who gave me the support I needed to dive into this sequel; you stimulated my desire to write . . .

To Estelle, my editor: your advice, attention, and tactful and sophisticated way of giving me your remarks will remain engraved in my writing.

To Guillaume . . . there is so much more I want to tell you, but it can't be written here . . . you had to embrace my exploration of Ireland; you made the sacrifice of being cold and drinking Guinness and whiskey there! I can tell you this now, even if I leave Diane to live her life without me from now on, we'll go back there . . .

To you, my readers, I am grateful and honored by your words, your encouragement, and your smiles . . .

To La Belle Hortense, for having given us the keys and allowed us to have a magnificent photo session there. The picture of Diane was taken in the place that inspired Happy People . . .

To Diane, the tiny little woman who came out of my imagination four years ago . . . you pushed me to write and gave me the gift of being an author . . . You will always have a special place in my heart . . .